Second-Best Friend

Second-Best Friend

ELIZABETH B. KEETON

Atheneum 1985 New York

LIBRARY OF CONGRESS CATALOGING IN PUBLICATION DATA

Keeton, Elizabeth B.
Second-best friend.

SUMMARY: When Vanessa borrows a dress from a friendless girl to wear to the seventh grade dance, not knowing the borrowed dress is stolen, she gains new insights into herself and other people.
1. Children's stories, American. [1. Friendship—Fiction] I. Title.
PZ7.K2516Se 1985 [Fic] 84-21561
ISBN 0-689-31096-X

Published simultaneously in Canada by
McClelland & Stewart, Ltd.
Composition by Yankee Typesetters,
Concord, New Hampshire
Printed and bound by Fairfield Graphics,
Fairfield, Pennsylvania
Designed by Marge Zaum
First Edition

To Bob,
who always found time
to read my daily writings.

Second-Best Friend

CHAPTER 1

"Cyclone" was not on Henrietta's mind. It was a hot and humid day—the twenty-eighth of August, 1933—and eerily still. The scorching wind that had blown all through the summer had suddenly stopped. Ominous weather! But not once did "cyclone" enter Henrietta's thoughts.

"Cyclone" danger in western Minnesota was usually over by late August. Besides, she had other things to worry about. Just this morning Pa'd said, "We don't get rain pretty soon, everything's gonna burn up." No crops meant no money for school clothes. Without new clothes, how could she hope to be popular at school?

More than anything Henrietta wanted to be

popular. She'd never been popular. Sometimes she had had popular friends—Eunice Anderson in third grade, for instance. And Clara, her present best friend, was popular—with the other farm girls, anyway. But none of her friends' popularity seemed to rub off on Henrietta.

Popularity was especially on Henrietta's mind because it was her birthday. She was twelve years old. "Getting into her teens," as Aunt Tillie put it. It had come over Henrietta while she was dressing this morning that being twelve marked a turning point in her life. What she was this year, she would be always.

But Aunt Tillie had been treating the day as if it were just any old day. All morning long it had been, "Go fill the water pail at the pump!" "Go get a pan of potatoes out of the cellar!" "Haven't you fed the chickens *yet?*"

So Henrietta had come to sit on the step outside the kitchen door where she could be by herself and think. The screen was covered with black flies, hiding her from Aunt Tillie in the kitchen. The flies came from the barnyard, which was no more than a hundred feet from the house.

But it was hard to think with Aunt Tillie's heavy steps going clump, clump right behind her, sometimes getting dangerously close to the screen. Aunt Tillie was very fat. "It's cuz I'm too good a cook," Aunt Tillie explained with a hearty laugh.

But Henrietta was wondering why, in that case, she and Pa, who'd been eating Aunt Tillie's cooking ever since Henrietta's mother died, stayed thin.

Suddenly Aunt Tillie was right at the screen yelling, "Henrietta! Come help get lunch! Henrietta Hanson!"

Henrietta slid off the step and huddled close to the wall.

"Where is that girl?" muttered Aunt Tillie, so close Henrietta could hear her wheezy breathing.

Aunt Tillie's heavy feet moved back into the kitchen. Pans banged on the stove. Then came the sizzling of grease in the frying pan.

Henrietta got back up on the step and stretched out her legs, wiggling her toes in the soft, warm dust. The step was very low, for the house sat on the ground. The house had no basement, just a tiny vegetable cellar that you got to by lifting a trapdoor in the middle of the kitchen floor.

The lowness of the step, along with the pool of dust in the bare spot in front of it, made the step just the right place to sit and think.

The thing that Henrietta was trying to figure out, as she wiggled her toes, was why, since she was smart at school lessons—a good deal smarter than Clara—she was so dumb when it came to talking to other kids.

Clara was always widening her eyes (an unpleasant little habit) and saying to her, "Don't you know *that?*"

But then, Clara heard things that Henrietta didn't hear. Clara had older brothers and sisters who talked in front of her.

It was hot on the step. Henrietta's eyes closed, until suddenly the step creaked and sagged beneath her. She opened her eyes with a start. But it was only Pa come in from the fields for lunch.

"Ain't you hot sitting in the sun?" asked Pa, raising a black cloud of flies as he opened the door.

Henrietta jumped to her feet. "Ya," she said, and slipped in at his heels.

"It's hot as blazes out in the fields," complained Pa, wiping the sweat from his face with his sopping wet sleeve. "Must be a hundred today."

Aunt Tillie looked up sharply from the potatoes she was frying. Her face was flushed from the heat of the wood cook stove. Sweat rolled down her fat cheeks. "It may be a hundred in here, but it ain't more'n eighty-five outdoors."

"It's more'n that," said Pa, taking off his hat and fanning his face with it.

"Go look for yourself."

Pa put his hat back on and went out the door to look at the thermometer nailed to the side of the house. Henrietta followed after him. She wanted Pa to be right. Not because she wanted Aunt Tillie to be wrong. There was security in the way Aunt Tillie was always right. It was just that nothing ever seemed to turn out right for Pa.

Pa's crops got planted too late. And so the frost got them. His horses went lame, and the cows dry. Even the old Model T Ford acted up on Pa, getting flat tires and running out of gas.

When Henrietta was little, the things that went wrong for Pa were so painful she'd had to run off somewhere and get down behind something, and rock back and forth until it didn't hurt so much; the way she did when she hit her finger with a hammer.

Now that she was big, she was over this "running off" business. Yet all kinds of little things—the thermometer disappointing Pa, for instance—made her feel anxious.

The thermometer read eighty-five. Neither Pa nor Henrietta said anything. They stood staring at the thermometer as if expecting it to change its mind and shoot upward.

"There's moisture in the air, that's for sure," said Pa at last. "Now if it'll just make into rain clouds."

A shadow passed over them. Henrietta looked up and saw a big cloud.

"There's a cloud," she sang out.

Pa squinted at the cloud. "Too white. There ain't enough moisture in it for rain." And he spit into the dirt in disgust.

All the way back to the door, Henrietta kept her eye on the cloud, marveling at the size of it. It was very fluffy. But the extraordinary thing about it was its height. It went up and up and up.

She didn't go inside with Pa. She stood on the step and watched the cloud sail majestically overhead. She'd never seen a cloud like this. She felt that a cloud so unusual—and on her birthday, too—must be up there for a special reason. Bring us rain! she silently begged.

From within the kitchen came the clatter of silverware. Pa and Aunt Tillie didn't wait around. Soon as food was cooked, they went right at it.

Her eyes still on the cloud, Henrietta absentmindedly opened the door wide to go in.

"You're letting in flies!" shrieked Aunt Tillie.

Henrietta hopped inside, slamming the door behind.

"You let in half a dozen," fussed Aunt Tillie.

Henrietta picked up the fly swatter and went after three big ones buzzing over the table.

"Let 'em be 'til we've done eating!" Aunt Tillie scolded, waving Henrietta away. "They'll fall in the food you hit 'em here!"

Henrietta put aside the swatter and took her place at the table. Pa and Aunt Tillie were already reaching for second helpings. They were fast eaters. They didn't talk. They just ate.

Henrietta wished they'd hold conversations at the table the way people did in books. Once she asked Clara, "Does your family talk when they eat?"

Clara answered, "Of course. Ma's always saying, 'I'm not gonna have you kids coming to the table like pigs to a trough.' "

It was a mistake to ask Clara questions about her home life. Clara's answers always left Henrietta feeling something was very wrong with the way she and Pa and Aunt Tillie lived.

To get a conversation going, Henrietta said, "Why don't we put the stove outdoors in the summer so it wouldn't get so hot in here?"

Pa, mopping up his plate with a piece of bread, only grunted.

Aunt Tillie, her mouth full, remembered, "Where was you when I needed help with lunch?"

So Henrietta gave up on conversation and let her eyes wander around the kitchen. It was where they did all their living.

The other downstairs rooms, the storage closet and the parlor, were not for "going into."

The storage closet, though big, was chuck full of all the things there wasn't room for anywhere else. If you didn't step carefully when you went in to fetch something, no end of things came tumbling down on you. The brooms, mops, pails, and carpentry tools were stored there. So were the washtubs, the clothes wringer, and the ironing board. And the shelves were packed with Aunt Tillie's cooking supplies. Just about everything she needed, except the flour. There was no room for the big flour barrel, so it stood in the corner by the kitchen cupboard.

The parlor was the prettiest room in the house. It was saved for company. Since company rarely came, Aunt Tillie kept her sewing machine in it. Right now she was making Henrietta a school dress out of printed flour sacks. The print was buttercup.

"There's already three buttercup dresses at school," Henrietta had complained.

"It just goes to show it's a popular pattern," Aunt Tillie had replied.

But the girls who wore the buttercup dresses were not popular. They were farm girls like Henrietta. Henrietta wanted to dress like the town girls in Eunice's group. And they never wore dresses made out of flour sacks.

It bothered Henrietta to see the parlor messy with flour sack cuttings. The floor was swept clean, though. Aunt Tillie liked to show off the linoleum. It was older than Henrietta, yet there wasn't a worn spot on it.

The kitchen linoleum was full of worn spots. But you couldn't tell. Rag rugs lay scattered about in such a way as to cover all the ugly spots. Henrietta noticed that a rug had gotten out of place. She jumped up from the table and put the rug back where it belonged.

Pa got up, too, and went out the door without saying anything.

Aunt Tillie rose and began taking things out of the storage closet. Baking powder and sugar, Henrietta noted. Things for her birthday cake.

Aunt Tillie always baked a birthday cake, and always the cake was a "surprise." When the cake was brought out from its hiding place behind the parlor sofa, you were supposed to act simply amazed, as if you had no idea.

Henrietta got right at the dishes. Aunt Tillie would want her out of the kitchen.

"I'll do the dishes," said Aunt Tillie, stooping before the stove to chuck in more wood. "Why don't you run on outdoors."

This was beginning to sound like a birthday! Henrietta had her hand on the screen when Aunt Tillie added, "You can water the vegetables."

Henrietta stared at Aunt Tillie in disbelief. "But it's my birthday!" she protested. "It's too hot out there now." And then, a happy thought, "I'll do it first thing in the morning!"

But Aunt Tillie's face stayed unrelenting. Holding onto her back to ease the kink in it, she straightened. "Tomorrow'll be too late! This hot sun's gonna burn 'em up. Now you get right on out there and water 'em."

"But—" started Henrietta, and then from the look in Aunt Tillie's eyes, gave up. She didn't see how one little afternoon was going to make any difference. But just try telling Aunt Tillie that! Feeling put upon, Henrietta opened the screen wide, forgetful of the flies clinging to it.

"You're letting in flies!" shrieked Aunt Tillie.

Henrietta hopped out. She stepped into a

brilliant patchwork of moving shadows and sunlight. Overhead a flotilla of fluffy clouds scudded across the sky, moving fast, in a hurry to get somewhere.

The big cloud was the teacher, Henrietta made up in her mind. Here come the pupils, hurrying to catch up. They got left behind because they stopped to play in the dirt.

She supposed though that Pa, out in the fields, was squinting at the clouds and saying, "Those dirty gray bottoms mean moisture."

Henrietta squinted at the clouds. "Not enough moisture for rain," she pronounced, and spit into the dirt.

Watering the garden was hard work. She had to lug water from the pump at the front of the house all the way around to the rear. Back and forth she trudged. She dripped sweat. It dropped from her nose and got into her mouth. As she worked, she didn't notice that the day was darkening. Her mind was on school—only eight days away.

She was thinking that this year she was going to be a different kind of girl—a "sure of herself" kind of girl. She simply wasn't going to let herself feel dumb around other kids. The trouble was, she seemed to say so many dumb things. The first day of school was the worst. That was because no kids her age lived anywhere near. There was nobody to talk to all summer long. So she got out of practice. And when she got back with kids again, she felt out of step. But she was sure that if she could just start school in a stunning new dress, then she wouldn't feel dumb at all.

Henrietta was at the well pumping water for the last row when she heard a rumble and looked up. The loose clouds that had gone scurrying through the sky seemed to have come together, crowding into a single jumble of dark clouds, jostling for places, pushing and bumping. Like the kids at school lining up to go in, mused Henrietta. So much activity made the great cloud look strangely alive.

"Bring rain for my birthday," pleaded Henrietta in a whisper that Aunt Tillie, close by in the kitchen with all the windows open, wouldn't hear.

The churning cloud answered with another rumble, a much louder rumble than the one seconds before. Lightning flashed across it like a snarl. The ferocity of the cloud startled Henrietta. There could be no connection between that first stately white cloud and this boiling dark mass.

She looked wearily at the vegetable garden. It didn't make sense to lug a pail all that way if it was going to rain anyhow. But supposing the storm suddenly veered in another direction. How awful it must feel, if you were a thirsty plant, to be abandoned just when your turn was next.

With a sigh she returned to the pump. Her flagging arms had the pail nearly full when she saw a cloud of dust coming down the field straight toward the barnyard. That would be Pa on the plow. Pa would be thirsty. She took the dipper from its hook, hung it on the rim of the pail, and went off at a trot, the water sloshing over onto her bare feet.

Pa drove the horses all the way to the barn before getting down off the plow. Sweat had caked the dust on his face, making the deep furrows in it look deeper than ever. Aunt Tillie was five years older than Pa. She was Pa's big sister. Yet Aunt Tillie's face was smooth.

Once Henrietta tried to talk to Aunt Tillie about this. "Why's Pa's face got wrinkles?" she worried. "Is it troubles that makes them?"

"Gracious! What a little worrywart you are! A few wrinkles ain't nothin'," was Aunt Tillie's response.

But looking up at Pa's lined face now, Henrietta felt a sudden pang. It was the things that went wrong for Pa that had done this to him, she was sure. If only, only it would rain! She dipped the dipper deep into the pail and brought it up brimming over.

Pa took the dipper without a word and gulped greedily. When he'd emptied it, he dipped a second dipper, and a third. Satisfied, he wiped his mouth with the back of his hand and grinned down at her. "I'm quitting," he said, tousling her damp locks with his big rough hand. "That cloud's gonna rain cats and dogs."

It's my birthday cloud," Henrietta informed him. She didn't feel afraid of the cloud anymore. She felt proud of it, as if its coming were entirely her doing.

For a few minutes they stood silently watching as the angry-looking cloud rolled toward them. Pa rested his back against the barn, his long legs crossed in front of him. Henrietta did the same, though she didn't find the position as comfortable as Pa seemed to.

The massive cloud was moving fast, blown along by the winds that churned its insides. As it neared, it seemed to grow blacker, and blacker, and blacker. Lightning streaked back and forth, sometimes from cloud to cloud, other times hurtling to the earth. The boom of thunder was almost constant.

The turbulence of the storm excited Henrietta. It made her want to run and to whoop, "It's gonna rain!" She grinned up at Pa. "It's like the Fourth of July fireworks, ain't it?"

But Pa wasn't grinning. His face, whitened with dust, looked ashen as he watched the storm come on—so near now Henrietta thought she could throw a stone and hit it. Suddenly Pa was on his feet. "There's a green tinge to that cloud! That means hail! Run to the house! Tell Aunt Tillie a bad storm's coming! I'll get the horses in!"

"What about the chickens?"

"Forget the chickens! Run!"

There was an urgency in Pa's voice that scared Henrietta. She ran as fast as she could. But not to the house. She ran to get the chickens in.

But the chickens seemed not to recognize the girl who came tearing into their yard waving her arms and shouting, "Shoo!" They squawked in fright and ran in every direction but toward the chicken house.

One ran out of the gate she'd left open. Henrietta ran after it. Rain was now coming down in big drops, drenching her, but she kept after the chicken, chasing it this way and that.

Suddenly it was black as night. Something hard hit Henrietta's head. Hail! She forgot the chicken, put her hands over her head and ran for the house, which was now closer than the chicken house.

In the flashes of lightning she saw Aunt Tillie at the kitchen door, holding it wide open, unmindful of flies. Aunt Tillie's mouth was opening and shutting. But a roaring—like an airplane flying low to get under the clouds—drowned out what Aunt Tillie was saying.

Just as Henrietta was within reach of the door, the wheelbarrow went sailing over her head. And a sudden rush of wind lifted her off her feet. But Aunt Tillie had hold of her. And Aunt Tillie pulled with a force that sent them both sprawling backwards into the kitchen.

As she went down, Henrietta saw that the trapdoor to the cellar stood open. "Cyclone!" flashed into her mind.

Terror sent Henrietta scrambling over Aunt Tillie. It sent her down the stepladder in such panic her foot missed a step, and she fell with a thud to the earthen floor. Clawing at the dirt, she rolled over against the stone wall.

It was pitch black in the cellar. The roaring was right there, right above her, sounding like a hundred freight trains roaring overhead. "I'm alone," Henrietta thought. "Pa and Aunt Tillie are up in the cyclone." She began to cry, and then her ears cracked; then felt as if they were going to blow out. She grabbed at them, covered them tightly with her hands.

Down in the blackness of the cellar, the roaring became not so loud. Then it was gone altogether. The only sound was the beating of rain against the house. Then that, too, stopped.

CHAPTER 2

Out of the blackness came Aunt Tillie's voice. "Where is everybody. I can't see nothin'."

"Right here. Standing beside you," said Pa's voice.

Henrietta's relief was so great she started crying again.

"You hurt?" came Pa's and Aunt Tillie's voices simultaneously.

"No."

"Why're you crying?"

"I dunno." Henrietta got to her feet and found Pa and Aunt Tillie in the blackness. She got between them and took hold of Aunt Tillie's dress with one hand and Pa's overalls with the other, feeling she never wanted to let go of them.

"We better not go up yet," said Aunt Tillie in a hushed voice. "We could be in the eye."

They waited, huddled about the ladder.

"It's over," declared Aunt Tillie, and started up, the ladder wrenching under her weight.

The trapdoor went up, letting light into the cellar. Aunt Tillie's feet disappeared into the kitchen. "God help us!" she cried out.

Pa went up the ladder so fast that Henrietta, close at his heels, got kicked. Pa didn't notice. Henrietta scarcely noticed, either.

The parlor was gone! Most of the wall on that side of the kitchen was gone! Henrietta looked out at a pile of rubble, and beyond that, at the open field. To her dazed eyes, the field looked different, as if the house had been carried off and set down in a strange place—somewhere she'd never been before.

But the thing that really held her attention was the wreckage at one side of the kitchen. It was as if a giant hand had ripped off a part of the house and crumbled it like a cracker.

She turned her eyes away from the sight, looked at the other side of the room where the stove and the table stood as if nothing had happened, pans and kettles on top of the stove, a coffee cup on the table. Even the rugs on that side were in place. But she found no comfort in this touch of normalcy. It just made the room look unreal.

Nobody spoke. Outside not a bird chirped. Not a breath of air stirred. We're the only ones left alive, crossed Henrietta's mind.

Aunt Tillie was the first to come out of shock. "Don't move!" she said to Henrietta. "There's glass everywhere. I'll get the broom." She waddled over to the storage closet, opened the door, and stared out into space.

For a moment Aunt Tillie just stood there staring. Then she turned and looked in bewilderment at Pa. "It's gone!"

That brought Pa to life. "The upstairs! I'll bet it's gone!" He went charging up the stairs.

Henrietta took a step after him and yelped in pain as glass cut into her bare feet.

"Stay where you are!" warned Aunt Tillie. "Bring down Henrietta her shoes!" she called up to Pa and started up the stairs herself, grunting heavily with each step—then had to step back down to make way for Pa, who came charging down, a pair of Aunt Tillie's shoes in his hands.

"Henrietta's room's gone!" said Pa, his voice sounding high and thin. "So's the roof! Everything's wet!" He handed Aunt Tillie's shoes to Henrietta. "Put these on!"

Henrietta stuck her feet into the shoes.

"They won't stay on," she complained, and shook a foot in the air to demonstrate, but the wet shoe hung on.

No one was paying attention to her. Pa and Aunt Tillie were in the doorway looking out at the barn.

"The cyclone didn't go out there. Everything out there's all right," Aunt Tillie was assuring Pa.

"I better go see!" said Pa and started off at a run. Halfway there he stopped, turned, and came running back, his eyes scared. "The corn's gone! The hail's wiped us out! We ain't got no corn, Tillie!"

Henrietta looked at the field. The corn was whittled down to stubs. She couldn't believe that what had just been there could be so suddenly all gone. She looked away, and then back again, as if to clear her vision. But the field stayed empty.

Aunt Tillie shaded her eyes with a hand and looked out over her glasses. "Ain't that some green way back there? Maybe it ain't so bad back a ways," she said, and started off to see for herself, though she only wore carpet slippers on her feet. Pa sprang after her. Henrietta followed behind, having a hard time keeping up in Aunt Tillie's big shoes.

They had gone only a little way when Pa said bitterly, "That green ain't ours. It's Old DeRuyter's."

Henrietta looked in dismay. It was so! The hail had stopped at the edge of their land, sparing Old DeRuyter's, though he had four times as much.

Old DeRuyter's farm was so big it completely surrounded the Hanson's hundred acres, shutting them off from their other neighbors. The DeRuyters weren't good neighbors. So sometimes Henrietta had the feeling she lived on an island.

Mrs. DeRuyter was from the old country and could speak little English. She stayed home and kept her house so spic and span you could eat off the floors. Old DeRuyter had a mean streak. Two years ago, the Hanson's cows broke through a fence and got into Old DeRuyter's corn. He came storming over, catching them at the table.

"A man who don't keep up his fences ain't no count!" he shouted at Pa.

Since then Pa and Aunt Tillie looked the other way when they passed Old DeRuyter on the street. But Henrietta stared straight at him, hoping he'd see her look of hate. She felt he'd insulted Pa, hurt his good name. And according to Aunt Tillie, Pa's good name was the only thing Pa had for sure. "Your Pa's got a good name," Aunt Tillie was always saying. "There ain't hard times or nothin' can take that away from him."

Looking now at the green on the other side of the fence, Henrietta felt that their ruined field wouldn't look quite so ruined if the DeRuyter field stood ruined alongside it. She knew this was a bad thought. But she couldn't help it! "Let's go home," she said.

But Pa and Aunt Tillie didn't seem to hear. They plowed on, their arms hanging at their sides like pieces of dead wood.

Suddenly Pa stopped. "What's that?"

He pointed at a strange creature sitting in the barren field. It had the shape of a large bird, but no feathers. It didn't get up and run away when they crowded around it.

"Why, it's one of our chickens! exclaimed Aunt Tillie. "Plucked clean by the cyclone."

"I'll be darned," said Pa.

"I don't see how the cyclone carried it out of the chicken yard," puzzled Aunt Tillie. "The cyclone didn't go in there."

Henrietta stared in horror. It had to be the chicken she had chased, the chicken that had gotten out because she left the gate open!

"I just don't see how the cyclone got it out of the chicken yard," Aunt Tillie kept puzzling.

Henrietta offered no explanation.

"This is one chicken I ain't gonna have to pluck before I cook it." Aunt Tillie reached for the chicken.

Henrietta was ahead of her, snatching the chicken from Aunt Tillie's outstretched hands. "We mustn't eat it!"

"I don't see why not. It's half dead now."

Henrietta wrapped her arms about the chicken. "We just mustn't!" She felt on the verge of tears.

Pa stepped between them. "Let her have the chicken, Tillie."

Pa and Aunt Tillie moved on, taking quick steps. It was past suppertime on the farm. The summer sun was getting low.

Henrietta stood where she was, not wanting to follow along, not wanting to return alone to the wrecked house, yet not wanting to just stand there, either.

She didn't know what to do with the chicken. She felt she should do something. Something to make up for leaving the gate open. Aunt Tillie was always saying, "Don't leave the gate open. Chickens ain't got the sense they was born with. They'll head for the highway and get hit by a car." This one had headed for the cyclone. Or had it been chased there?

Pa and Aunt Tillie looked far away, but Aunt Tillie's voice came back clearly in the still evening air. She was fussing at Pa. "You know perfectly well that chicken's gonna die! It ain't no kindness to the chicken! And it ain't no kindness to Henrietta!"

Henrietta looked in alarm at the chicken. "Don't die!"

The chicken stared back vacantly through glazed eyes.

"I won't let you die," said Henrietta, and pressed the chicken close to her chest, as if to give it life from herself. She started back to the house, the clopping of the too-big shoes the only sound in the ruined field.

As long as she was with Pa and Aunt Tillie, the field had looked barren, but at least it had been their *very own* barren field. Alone in it, she felt it to be an alien field, belonging to nobody. A feeling of desolation swept over her.

And the house, as she neared it, gave no comfort. A gaping hole let her look into the kitchen. And the upstairs hallway was bared for anyone out on the highway to see. It didn't look like her house, anymore. It looked like an abandoned house where nobody lived.

It was brighter inside the kitchen than usual at this time of evening. The last rays of the setting sun poured through the huge hole in the wall. But the brightness didn't cheer. It lit up the shattered glass on the floor, the shredded curtains, the heap of rubble.

Henrietta stood in the kitchen doorway, unwilling to enter. A sudden gust of cool wind swept over her, rattled the calendar on the wall, and passed on out through the hole.

"Summer's over," the wind seemed to be saying. "Get ready for fall."

But what was the chicken going to do without any feathers? Henrietta started up the stairs in search of something in Aunt Tillie's ragbag that could be made into a dress.

The stairway, ordinarily dark even with the sun out, seemed oddly lighted. She looked up, up into the sky. Then she remembered her room wouldn't be there. She didn't want to see. It was spooky going up alone. She hesitated. But returning to the darkening kitchen was spooky, too. Hugging the chicken she continued up the stairs.

At the top she gasped. Her room had disappeared. She hadn't expected it would be *all* gone. Her clothes gone. Her treasures gone. Everything she owned gone.

She turned away, went into Aunt Tillie's room, which was all there, just the ceiling gone. The ragbag was soaked; but she found a piece of yellow taffeta she didn't think was too wet and began fastening it around the chicken with safety pins.

But it was hard to see. She mistook a finger for cloth and stuck herself. There was a bad feeling inside her that was getting worse by the minute. So she tucked the chicken under her arm, its dress hanging loose, and went downstairs.

She sat in the old kitchen rocker and rocked back and forth with all her might. The chair seemed at times in danger of pitching over. Glass crunched beneath the rockers. The sound was an appropriate accompaniment.

Lots of times, when Henrietta felt bad about something, all she had to do was rock in the old rocker, and pretty soon things seemed all right again. But this time the rocking only jiggled up the bad feeling inside her.

She'd done a terrible thing! She'd run for the cellar. She'd given no thought to Aunt Tillie lying on the floor. She'd climbed over her. Aunt Tillie had held the door open for her, had pulled her in. Yet she'd thought only of herself. She hadn't known she was like that! She'd always supposed that, put to the test, she'd be a heroine.

A sound at her back sent her spinning round in the rocker. A face was at the window. Immediately the face disappeared. But not before Henrietta recognized Roland DeRuyter, Old DeRuyter's grandson.

Roland was in her grade. He'd come as a new boy last April, from Minneapolis. He was unlike anybody Henrietta had ever known.

For one thing, he had straight black hair and black eyes and skin that stayed tan through the winter. He stood out in a room full of Scandinavian blonds.

And he was—well, distant. He had a way of not looking at anyone, as if he were the only one around. And the corners of his mouth turned down—like an old person's. It made him look haughty, as if he had no use for anybody else.

Clara said Roland was "stuck up." But Henrietta thought it might just be that people in a big city were like that.

Henrietta forgave him right off for being a DeRuyter because his mother had died, like hers. She thought it gave them something in common. To be sure, his mother had died only six months ago. She could barely remember Ma. And, of course, she had Aunt Tillie, while Roland had a new stepmother. Still, they were the only ones in the room without real mothers.

Then something happened to make her afraid of Roland DeRuyter. It happened in town one Saturday afternoon when she was on her way to Mrs. Swensen's with a pail of eggs. She was passing a house with an angry mother in it. "Laziest boy I ever saw!" the mother scolded. "It's in the blood!"

At that, a boy's yell rose above the scolding. "Damn you!"

That brought Henrietta to a standstill. It brought the whole house to a standstill. There wasn't a sound in it. Then the scolding started up again. "Just wait 'til your pa gets home!"

Suddenly the door banged open and out came Roland carrying a heavy slop pail. When he saw Henrietta standing there, he scowled as if he'd caught her snooping. Then he threw the slop in her direction.

It splashed her up to the knees. She ran all the way to Mrs. Swensen's. When Mrs. Swensen opened the pail, half of the eggs were broken. "I can't pay but half price for the unbroken eggs," Mrs. Swensen said, "because I'm going to have to clean them up."

"Stay away from them DeRuyters," Aunt Tillie cautioned when Henrietta explained why there wasn't much egg money. "Old DeRuyter's got a mean streak in him, and I expect his grandson has, too. Just don't have nothin' to do with 'em."

Voices! Right outside the window. Henrietta crept to the window. Old DeRuyter stood beside his car talking to Pa and Aunt Tillie. Roland was there, too, leaning against the car, his face turned away as if he found listening to Hanson troubles tiresome.

Finally Old DeRuyter and Roland got into the car. Doors slammed. The big car glided out of the driveway. Pa and Aunt Tillie moved toward the house. Henrietta quickly got back into the rocker.

"It's funny we was the only ones that cloud dropped a cyclone on," said Pa, coming through the door.

"I don't know what we done that we was the only ones," fretted Aunt Tillie, close behind.

Henrietta, remembering she'd wished for the cloud to come—and a birthday wish, at that—scrunched deeper into the rocker.

"Whatcha just sitting for?" said Aunt Tillie crossly.

Pa's face looked drawn. He sat down in a chair and stared at where the wall was gone. Outside the cows were bawling to be milked. But Pa didn't seem to hear them.

"Get that chicken out of here!" said Aunt

Tillie, spotting it, though Henrietta had her hands over it.

"It can't walk. I think something's broken."

"I told you that chicken was hurt too bad to live. Now take it out to the chicken house where it belongs."

Henrietta cast a pleading glance over at Pa. But he sat immobile. So she got up out of the rocker, and with a "How can you be so mean?" backward look at Aunt Tillie, went out the door.

In the chicken house the chickens were already up on the roosts. She put the chicken in a nest and ran to the haystack for straw to cover it. When she returned, the chicken was out of the nest and trying to flap its way up onto a roost with featherless wings.

"You can walk!" Henrietta cried out joyously. "You're gonna live!"

She picked the chicken up and cuddled it in her arms as she carried it back to the nest. She'd save it from being eaten! Such a life-saving feat made up for abandoning it, for abandoning Aunt Tillie. It turned her into an "all right" girl again.

"Now you stay here. Don't be scared. I won't let nobody get you," she promised, tucking the straw about it.

But she no sooner turned her back than the

chicken was out of the nest. She gave up and put it on a pole alongside the other chickens.

On the way to the house, she saw Pa come out of the kitchen and head for the barn, milk pails in hand. "The chicken's feelin' better!" she called out to him.

But the cows were bellowing desperately. And so maybe Pa didn't hear her. He passed her silently.

Inside the kitchen Aunt Tillie had lit the lamp and moved it over to the stove. It put the rest of the kitchen in shadow. She was trying to fix supper, letting out little cries of distress each time the thing she needed—first lard, then sugar—turned out to have been kept in the storage closet, now lost for good.

Henrietta stood in the doorway and said, "The chicken's gonna live. It can walk."

But Aunt Tillie, not able to find the salt, paid no attention.

Henrietta went back into the rocker. It's my birthday, she suddenly remembered. But what good was a birthday when everyone but you had forgotten about it?

A mosquito whined in her ear. She was unable to lift an arm to swat at it. She felt heavy, so heavy she could scarcely move her feet to keep the rocker in motion.

Over at the stove Aunt Tillie grabbed up a dish towel and flipped it at the moths fluttering around the lamp. "Your pa better get in here quick so we can eat and put out this light," she said. "Every bug for miles around is gonna head straight for our kitchen where they can fly right in."

"If they're miles away," said Henrietta, her voice sounding small and far away in her ears, "how do they know they can fly right in?"

If Henrietta got an answer, she didn't hear it. The rocker stopped altogether. She was asleep.

She woke up with a start and found herself in Pa's arms going up the stairs. Somewhere in the background Aunt Tillie was saying, "This hall closet emptied of its things will do nicely for a bedroom."

Pa carried her into the closet and laid her on a blanket spread out on the floor. The moment Henrietta's head touched the pillow, she was back asleep.

CHAPTER 3

Henrietta woke up in the morning to the sound of voices out in the yard. She jumped up and peered down through the jagged hole where her room used to be. Men milled about the yard, mostly farmers who lived nearby, though Mr. Nelson from the lumber yard was there. So was Old DeRuyter and his hired man, and Roland.

Old DeRuyter was taking charge, telling the men how to go about putting up a blown-down telephone pole. A group of neighboring farmers had put up the telephone line themselves back in 1903, and it still belonged to them. But it looked as if the men meant to do something about the house, too.

Old DeRuyter must've gone home and called everybody up he could, decided Henrietta. He must've said, "If it rains, it'll come right in. We got to get a roof over their heads." She supposed she'd have to like Old DeRuyter now.

And everybody had turned out! That must mean everybody liked them. She'd been worrying about that. In town Pa never joined the groups of farmers standing on corners discussing weather and crops. He tended to his business. And when that was done, he stood by himself at the car, one foot on the fender, and waited for Aunt Tillie and Henrietta to show up.

Aunt Tillie, on the other hand, started talking the moment she set foot on Main Street. Mostly she talked about herself.

"I take the littlest, bitty stitches you ever saw," she bragged to the bored-looking clerk at the yardage counter, forgetting she'd bragged about that the last time she was in.

And Aunt Tillie liked to argue about the prices. "Cabbage is five cents a pound down the street at Al's Market," she complained at Olson's Grocery. "So how come you got yours priced at six cents?"

Some men set a ladder against the house. Henrietta ducked back into the closet to put on her clothes. To her surprise, she saw that she was dressed. Then she remembered that the clothes on her back were all she had. And she was wearing her very worst everyday dress! It was faded and had a patch at the back from going over a barb wire fence. It was dirty from the cellar floor and crumpled from sleeping in.

Well, she thought, as she started down the stairs, when people look at me, I'll just say, "I can't help this dress. The cyclone blew away all my clothes. So it's all I have 'til we get to the store." She felt important.

Three neighbor women had come with baskets of food to help Aunt Tillie get lunch for the workers. But they didn't look at Henrietta when she came into the kitchen. Their eyes were glued to Aunt Tillie. Aunt Tillie was telling about the cyclone.

Henrietta found a pan of cold corn meal mush at the back of the stove. But when she went to get a bowl and spoon out of the cupboard, she saw that Mrs. Johnson stood in front of it. Mrs. Johnson had four girls of her own, all grown now. To hear Mrs. Johnson tell it, her girls—unlike Henrietta—worked from morning 'til night without complaint. Once Henrietta overheard Mrs. Johnson say to Aunt Tillie, "Tillie, you're gonna ruin that girl the way you spoil her!"

Henrietta was afraid if she asked Mrs. Johnson to move, Mrs. Johnson would say, "What! You just getting up? My girls would of been up and *cooked* breakfast long before this!" So Henrietta took the pan and sat down in a corner and ate with her fingers.

"And there was Henry and Henrietta racing the cyclone," Aunt Tillie was telling: "Him coming from one direction and her from the other, both of 'em running like jack rabbits, and me holding the door open and thinking, 'They ain't gonna make it!' "

Henrietta felt eyes turning on her. She stared hard into the pan. The bad feeling was still inside her. All it took were the words, "holding the door open" to bring it back full force.

"It was a miracle none of us got hurt," went on Aunt Tillie, having the time of her life. "We was that close, but that cyclone didn't touch a hair on our heads. Didn't touch none of the animals, neither, except one poor chicken that got plucked clean as a whistle."

Her chicken! She'd forgotten it! Henrietta jumped to her feet.

Aunt Tillie broke off her story. "Where you going?"

"To see my chicken."

"I took it out of the chicken yard. The other chickens was pecking it to death."

That so alarmed Henrietta she raced off, paying no heed to Aunt Tillie's, "Come back and get shoes on! There's glass and nails everywhere!"

The chicken was pacing jerkily back and forth in front of the gate. The dress had fallen off, or been pecked off. It hung by a shred, trailing behind. The chicken's head kept making little darts at the fence, as if it kept thinking it saw a hole it could squeeze through. It walked so lopsided it looked in danger of toppling over, and it was bloodied from the pecking.

"Oh," gasped Henrietta. It was all she could do not to turn and run from the sight of it. But she felt she must do something for it. She ran to the granary and came back with a handful of oats, which she scattered over the chicken, the kernels bouncing off its head. But the chicken ignored the grain.

She ran to the kitchen and got a saucer without anyone noticing—Aunt Tillie was still going on about the cyclone—and filled the saucer at the pump. Then she ran fast as she could to the chicken, losing a good deal of water over the sides, and set the saucer in the chicken's path. But the chicken walked right over it, one foot landing smack in the middle of the saucer. Henrietta got down on her knees and forced the chicken's beak into the water. But it wouldn't drink. Despairing, she let the chicken go and got slowly to her feet.

"It don't look so good."

Startled, Henrietta swung around.

Roland DeRuyter stood behind her, soberly studying the chicken. He put out a foot. The chicken ran right into it. "It don't see so good, neither."

Henrietta was so glad to find someone on whom she could unburden herself about the chicken, she forgot all about the DeRuyter mean streak. "It won't eat. And it won't drink," she told him. "It wants in the chicken yard, but the other chickens won't let it because the cyclone pulled out all its feathers. I don't know what to do for it."

Roland raised his eyes from the chicken and looked at Henrietta. From the way he was looking at her, Henrietta thought he wanted to be friends. Instead he turned his back on her and stood leaning against the fence, one foot stuck between the wires.

She wondered if he was lonely. He had no friends. That was his doing, though. From the first, everybody had liked his dark good looks. But it wasn't easy to be friendly with somebody who acted as if he didn't want anything to do with you. Henrietta moved up beside him and stuck her foot between the wires—like his. It seemed the friendly thing to do.

Up close, his mouth—which she'd thought of in the classroom as a sneering mouth—didn't look sneering. The corners were still pulled down. They'd probably grown that way by now. But it looked a tight, unhappy mouth, nothing more.

Roland placed his arms on top the fence, stretched them out as if to rest them.

But Henrietta saw that by so doing, his arms partially hid his face. He knows I'm looking, she thought. It makes him shy. She'd not supposed such a proud boy could be shy.

She placed her arms on top the fence, too, and leaned a bit forward so he could see she wasn't looking anymore.

The fence was too high. It was uncomfortable keeping her arms on top of it. Roland could do it because he was taller. He was taller because he was older. She'd seen the little pink card that came with new pupils when she went up to the teacher's desk with a late paper. Roland was thirteen, had been thirteen since last April.

She let one arm drop. Then the other.

His eyes not moving from the chickens, Roland said, "You ain't tall enough."

It was the wrong thing to say. Henrietta did a lot of worrying that she was going to be short like Aunt Tillie. She came back at Roland with, "I could do it now if I was thirteen years and four months old."

It was as if she'd slapped him. A dull red spread over his tanned cheeks, making them look coppery.

Henrietta was sorry. She hadn't meant to offend him. To make amends, she said, "There's nothing wrong with staying back a year. Lots of kids do. There's two besides you in our room that're thirteen."

That didn't help. The red spread to his ears.

Now he'll go away, worried Henrietta.

But Roland stayed at the fence, his dark eyes brooding over the chickens. Then unexpectedly he said—to the chickens as far as Henrietta could tell—"The reason I'm old for my grade is because my ma started me late. She was afraid the other kids would pick on me because I'm half Sioux Indian."

Of course! The black hair. The nearly black eyes. Henrietta found it hard not to stare now that she saw "Indian" so plainly. To think that all these years Young DeRuyter had been living in Minneapolis with a Sioux Indian wife. And nobody knew. Old DeRuyter never told. But Roland was telling. What would Old DeRuyter say to that?

Old DeRuyter was a hard man. He had been so hard on Young DeRuyter people still talked about it. "Hard on him when he was a boy," they said. "And hard on him when he was grown. Old DeRuyter's hard on them that don't do what he wants."

But Henrietta, stealing a glance at it, thought that Roland's pulled down mouth looked as if it did what *it* wanted, no matter. She asked, "Did kids pick on you?"

For a moment she thought he wasn't going to answer. Then his black eyes, looking every bit as hard as Old DeRuyter's gray ones, flashed at her. "They didn't dare. I was bigger."

She was on touchy ground. Roland's look said so. There was another question she wanted to ask. She felt bursting to ask it. But she shut her mouth tightly and put her attention on the chickens, which were peacefully scratching the ground for tasty tidbits.

How could it be that these chickens, her very own chickens that she fed and watered and even shoveled out their manure—at least, she would shovel it out if Aunt Tillie didn't keep getting impatient and beat her to it—would go after a poor, bald chicken?

"I didn't know they was so mean!" burst out of her.

Roland's eyes narrowed on the chickens. He looked as if he could wring the neck of every one of them. "Oh, they're mean all right! Just let one of them be different, and they don't want it around!"

Out popped the question. "Did people not want your ma around?"

The narrowed eyes were suddenly on her, as if they saw another chicken. Then he was gone, taking long strides toward the house.

Now she'd done it! What had gotten into her, anyway! And after she'd made up her mind *not* to say it! He'd not want her for a friend now. But she wanted to be his friend, she suddenly felt; she wanted him for a friend more than she wanted any other kid she knew. "Wait!" she called, and ran after him.

But he ran too, and the faster she ran, the faster he ran. And when she neared the house, Aunt Tillie came out holding up her shoes. "They found your shoes in the rubble!"

Henrietta took the shoes without pleasure. A year ago Aunt Tillie had bought them extra big. "Now that you're eleven, you'll probably grow a lot," she'd said. "You don't wanna outgrow 'em before you outwear 'em."

But here she was twelve. And the shoes, though badly scuffed, were still too big. She was afraid they were going to last all through seventh grade. She said, "I wish the cyclone'd blown them away!"

A cluck of disapproval came from the doorway. Henrietta looked up and saw Mrs. Johnson standing there. Mrs. Johnson's disapproving look as much as said, "My daughters never complained about their shoes!"

Henrietta shoved her feet into the shoes and went off to look for Roland. She spotted him helping some men unload a wagon of lumber. She kept an eye on him. And when the men left him to finish the job alone, she wandered over and stood beside the wagon.

But Roland acted as if he didn't see her standing there. He went on with the unloading, tossing out planks in a careless, easy way, moving on cat's feet.

Because he's wearing tennis shoes, thought Henrietta. She wondered what Old DeRuyter thought of tennis shoes, which were no good at all around barnyard manure. Old DeRuyter wore heavy leather shoes that came over the ankle. And he wore overalls like the other farmers. Roland wore new-looking blue jeans. A red handkerchief was tied loosely around his neck, the way cowboys in movies wore them. He looked dandified next to the roughly dressed farmers.

It was awkward standing there, in plain sight yet unseen. Henrietta tried to think of something to say. But it was hard to think of anything when it was as if you weren't there. Finally she said, "You look like you could use a helper."

A plank landed within inches of her feet. It reminded her of the slop pail. Aunt Tillie was right. The DeRuyters had a mean streak. It was best to stay away from them.

But the day was spoiled. There wasn't much to do. What she did wasn't fun. Staying away from Roland didn't leave many places to go.

She stood looking up at the roofers. "Look out!" they yelled as old shingles came rattling down.

She perched herself on the kitchen stool and listened to the talk of the women. "If you ain't got nothin' to do," said Aunt Tillie, "come dry the dishes."

*

She went up to Aunt Tillie's room and stood a long time before the mirror hanging over Aunt Tillie's dresser. It was a small mirror and was full of specks, making her look as if she had chickenpox.

She was wondering if being twelve years old had changed the way she looked. It was hard to tell.

She had no trouble telling that Eunice, with her long red hair and big brown eyes, was pretty. Nor that Clara, with her blonde curls and blue eyes, was. But with herself she had to depend on what other people said.

And last summer in the drugstore, an out-of-towner—a traveler stopping for a cold drink—had pointed at her and said to his companion, "What a homespun look that little girl has about her."

Henrietta had gone immediately to the dictionary to find out *exactly* what "homespun" meant. She found a number of descriptive words:

"of unaffected simplicity", "unsophisticated," and "plain." None of them sounded good. She especially disliked the thought of being considered "plain." It sounded so ordinary.

To be sure, once in town when the wind was blowing her hair all over, a man stopped her to say, "Little girl, what a head of hair you've got!" That was because there was lots of it. But what good was lots of it, if it was brown and straight?

And another time a clerk in a store said, "What nice eyes." Not "pretty." Just "nice." Her eyes weren't any particular color. When she wore blue, people said she had blue eyes. When she wore brown, they called her brown-eyed. She didn't know if that was nice or not.

But maybe it wasn't so much *how* you looked—hair and eyes and things like that. Maybe it was what you wore. Both Eunice and Clara wore pretty dresses. Maybe in plain dresses they'd look plain, too.

It was hot up in Aunt Tillie's room. Flies came in through the openings. They buzzed around Henrietta's face. She started down the stairs.

Halfway down, just out of sight of the kitchen, she heard, "Too bad he can't get along with his new stepma."

Henrietta stopped where she was, having learned that interesting talk had a way of breaking off when she came into the room.

"Well," said another voice, "I expect the old

folks are glad to have him. I hear tell the old man's taken a liking to the boy."

There was silence.

Thinking the talk over, Henrietta went on down.

"Looks like the pa don't know how to pick a wife," took up the first voice. "I heard the first one was a —"

The talk stopped short. Henrietta was seen.

Henrietta sidled up to Aunt Tillie. "Is Roland gonna live with the Old DeRuyters?" she asked in a hushed voice.

"That's what they say," answered Aunt Tillie in her hearty voice.

"For always," whispered Henrietta.

"They say so," boomed Aunt Tillie.

Henrietta turned away from Aunt Tillie in despair. Roland would be riding *her* bus! She had enough bus troubles without adding Roland. Nothing was going right! This was turning out to be the most disagreeable day of her life!

At last evening came. One by one the farmers got in their cars and went home to chores. Pa had chores to do himself and went off to the barn. But Aunt Tillie stood out in the yard thanking everyone, saying over and over, "It's a miracle what you done."

Henrietta saw no miracle. The roof was on.

The torn-away side was boarded up. And glass had been put in the windows. But that was all. The house looked chopped off. It looked like a granary.

When the last farmer had departed, Henrietta turned to Aunt Tillie. "Are they coming back tomorrow?"

"Goodness gracious no! This is a busy time for farmers. What'd they want to come back for?"

"But what about my bedroom? And what'll we use for a parlor if we get company?"

"Be thankful the cyclone left as much as it did. You fed the chickens yet?"

Her chicken! She'd forgotten it again! Henrietta raced off to the chicken yard.

She found the chicken sitting in front of the gate. It looked dumpy. She picked it up. It felt like a bunch of bones in her hands.

Not knowing what to do with it, she carried it under her arm while she fed the chickens. "You take a peck at it," she yelled at the chickens, "and you're gonna get kicked!"

But the chickens were interested only in the grain she scattered about.

Still not knowing what to do with the chicken, Henrietta carried it into the house with her.

Aunt Tillie was at the stove heating up leftovers. "Get that chicken out of here!" she said without looking up.

"It's got no place to go."

"The kitchen's no place for it!"

"It's not eaten. It won't make droppings."

"Not in my kitchen, it won't!"

Henrietta went out the door and sat on the step. She let the chicken lie in her lap without touching it or looking at it. It seemed, suddenly, a terrible burden—something she was never going to know what to do with.

"Whatcha doing out here?" asked Pa, coming from the barn with a pail of milk in each hand.

Henrietta looked up at Pa. "The chicken ain't eaten all day. It won't make droppings. But Aunt Tillie won't let it in."

Pa went into the house without saying anything.

"Supper!" called Aunt Tillie.

"I can't come in. I got no place to put the chicken," Henrietta answered stubbornly.

She heard the sound of chairs being pulled up to the table. Then the clash of silverware. They were eating without her! Her eyes filled with tears.

A chair scraped the floor. Pa stepped to the

door. "Why don'tcha put the chicken in the granary for the night? With all that grain around, maybe it'll eat somethin'."

That sounded like a good idea. Henrietta ran off to the granary with the chicken.

It was dark inside. She pushed the door as wide open as possible to let the twilight in.

When she put the chicken on the floor, it flopped limply over on its side. She saw with horror that its mouth was open and its eyes shut. Dead!

She ran out of the granary and pounded over the barnyard as hard as she could to the house. She was out of breath when she got there.

The lamp was lit. Pa and Aunt Tillie sat under its light doing some figuring on paper. Henrietta filled a plate and sat down at the opposite end of the table, where her face was in shadow. She felt possessed of a guilty secret. All anybody had to do to discover it was to look at her face, she was sure.

The food that had smelled so good when Aunt Tillie was cooking it didn't look good now that she had it in front of her. Henrietta pushed the plate away.

"We got to buy washtubs," Aunt Tillie was saying. "And an ironing board. They was all in the storage closet."

"And dresses for me," put in Henrietta.

"They can wait," said Aunt Tillie, not taking her eyes off the paper. "And a clothes wringer," she went on to Pa. "I can do without a sewing machine, but I got to have a clothes wringer."

"But I don't have nothin' to wear to school."

"School ain't here yet. Put down broom. Emma Johnson will want hers back." Aunt Tillie looked up anxiously at Pa. "I still got a lot of canning down in the cellar. It'll get us through the winter. But we're gonna be needing potatoes and sugar and things like that from the store."

Pa's chin went up a bit. "We ain't so poor we can't buy them things. Us farmers'er better off than them town folks. We got our land to grow things on. We got our cows and chickens. We got our own telephone line us farmers put up ourselves. Ain't nobody can do nothin' to us so long as we don't go and put a mortgage on our farm to buy things we can't pay for."

"I don't have nothin' to wear when we go to town Saturday," piped up Henrietta.

Aunt Tillie looked at Henrietta over her glasses. "Girl, you better get used to making do with what you got. There just ain't gonna be money to buy nothin'."

Henrietta was shocked. Were they really

going to be poor—like the Strouts, who wore cast-off clothes given to them by the people Mrs. Strout washed for? She hid her face in her hands. She didn't think she could bear to be poor.

Aunt Tillie peered over her glasses again. "You look plum tuckered out. You better go on up to bed. Leave your dress down here, and I'll wash and iron it. If you look clean and well mended, folks are gonna respect you no matter what you got on."

Grownups maybe. But not kids! Henrietta took off the dress and went wearily up the stairs.

Stretched out on the blanket, she felt the hard floor underneath. She turned from back to stomach and from side to side. In fact she kept turning, it seemed to her, all night long.

She woke up in the morning feeling she hadn't slept at all. How did they expect her to be smart in school if she didn't have a comfortable place to sleep? She saw that her dress, freshly washed and ironed, was hanging on the door-knob. Full of resentment, she put it on. There was money for a broom and a washtub, but nothing for her!

Going down the stairs, she saw in her mind the chicken lying lifeless on the granary floor, bald and bloodied. She didn't want to see it. She tried to think of something else.

At the bottom, as she brushed past the hook by the door, all the coats fell off. They always did that! You'd think there'd be somewhere else to hang them!

She stooped for the coats. Four coats hanging on one hook! No wonder they came off! She picked up her winter coat.

Not turning from the window she was washing, Aunt Tillie said, "It's a good thing your coat was left on that hook."

All summer long Aunt Tillie'd been after her, "For goodness sakes! Take that winter coat up to your room!" Henrietta felt she should point out to Aunt Tillie how lucky it was she hadn't listened to her. But she didn't have the energy. She slumped into a chair and laid her head in her arms down on the table.

The glass squeaked plaintively under Aunt Tillie's rag. "Your pa looked in on the chicken this morning. It was dead. So he buried it."

And just when she'd stopped thinking about it!

"I told you that chicken wasn't gonna live."

That was too much! It was simply too much! Henrietta jumped up and ran for the door.

Aunt Tillie turned from the window. "Where you going?"

The screen open—letting the flies in—Henrietta flung at Aunt Tillie, "You made it die all alone out in that dark granary!"

Then she was off and running, across the barnyard, through the stubby corn, all the way to the big boulder at the edge of the cornfield.

Sitting in the boulder's shade, her back resting against the hard stone, she felt utterly dissatisfied with herself. She had told a fib to Aunt Tillie. The chicken hadn't died alone in the granary. It was dead before it got there. She had said it to make Aunt Tillie feel bad. She was turning into an awful girl! No wonder nobody liked her!

She didn't used to be like this. Kids used to like her. Back in the third grade the most popular girl in the room, Eunice Anderson, was her best friend. Though, in a way, she bought Eunice's friendship.

Eunice sat behind her. So she let Eunice copy her school papers. She didn't know it was wrong. She thought she was being nice. Eunice said she was. Every time Eunice got back a paper with an A on it, Eunice said, "You're the nicest friend I ever had."

But they were careful not to let Miss Jackson see them, Henrietta remembered. So maybe she had known it was wrong. And eventually Miss Jackson did see them. "You're cheating!" she accused them right in front of the class.

At recess Eunice stormed at Henrietta, "Now Miss Jackson doesn't like me. And it's *your* fault!"

Henrietta stormed back. "You asked me! You'd of been mad at me if I wouldn't of!"

The quarrel broke up their friendship. The next year Eunice found other friends, town girls. She'd had little to do with Henrietta since.

"Henrietta!" came Aunt Tillie's call, sounding faint in the wind, which blew it away.

Henrietta sat rigid, as if the least movement might disclose her hiding place.

Aunt Tillie stopped calling. Then there was no sound. Just the moaning of the wind.

Atop the boulder, a meadow lark burst suddenly into song.

Henrietta got stealthily to her feet. The bird heard her and flew off.

"I won't hurt you!" Henrietta called after it.

But the bird flew on.

Henrietta watched until the bird was out of sight. Then she started back to the house—not running, her usual way of getting from place to place—walking slowly, deep in thought.

She was thinking she'd make it up to Aunt Tillie. She wouldn't say anything to make Aunt Tillie feel bad. She wouldn't complain about having only one dress, even if it was an old, everyday dress.

Cinderella had had only one dress, Henrietta suddenly remembered. And it was an old, everyday dress, too. And look what happened to Cinderella!

Henrietta broke into a run, her feet leaping over the sharp stubs, the wind whistling in her ears. She felt all at once light and free and joyous. She was a new girl—a heroic kind of girl—with all sorts of wonderful things waiting to happen to her.

Aunt Tillie was waiting at the kitchen door. "Look what Emma Johnson brung over while you was gone," she said, pointing to a heap of old clothes on the table. "She brung you some things her girls don't wear no more."

Henrietta was incredulous. "The Johnson girls are old. One's married.

"Nellie's still in high school. There's two dresses that ain't been worn hardly."

Henrietta stayed incredulous. "They're women's dresses. They won't fit."

"I can cut 'em down."

"They'll still look like women's dresses!"

"Nonsense. Cut down nobody'll know." Aunt Tillie held up a purple dress with gold and blue stripes zigzagging up and down it. "This here purple's hardly been worn at all."

"Because nobody would wear it!"

"Then there's this green." Aunt Tillie held up a green dress with funny little yellow triangles all over it. "It's got a hole where one of the girls must of caught it on somethin', but I can cut the hole out when I cut it down."

"Nellie rides my bus. She'll tell everybody, 'There goes my green dress that I got a hole in and Ma gave to the Hansons.' "

"Nobody'll think nothin' of it. Everybody knows your room got blown away."

"They will too! They'll think we're poor!" cried Henrietta, and—though she didn't exactly mean to—stamped her foot.

"I never seen a girl so hard to please!" Aunt Tillie's chin quivered. She looked as if she might cry.

Henrietta felt ashamed of herself. And right after she'd made up her mind to be nice to Aunt Tillie, too. She turned and went up the stairs to the closet. But it's cramped darkness only accentuated her woes. So she sat down on the top step, chin cupped in hands, and tried to figure things out.

Was she being punished for not talking to Ida Strout last year in school? But nobody talked to Ida, who was big and slow, and took two years to get through a grade. Since Ida was the oldest of the Strout kids—there were eight of them—Ida wore the cast-off women's dresses. They fit her badly. And she looked like a grown woman in them.

Eunice said it gave her the willies to see what looked like a woman in their grade. After Eunice said that, everybody got the willies.

But I felt sorry for Ida, Henrietta remembered. I didn't say anything mean to her. But then, nobody really said anything mean to Ida. They just ignored her.

Down in the kitchen there was a sudden commotion: Pa coming in the door with a lot of thumps and bumps and grunts. "Where's Henrietta?" he called out. "I've bought somethin' for her!"

From the gladness in Pa's voice, Henrietta knew it was something good. She thought it might be a new dress. She ran down the stairs. But it was only an old iron cot. When Pa put it in the closet, there wasn't room left to walk around.

"I picked it up for a buck at the foreclosure auction over to Harmons' farm," said Pa proudly.

Henrietta's disappointment was terrible. But she pretended to be glad. She gave Pa a hug.

In bed that night, lying perfectly still—the cot squeaked horrendously if she moved—Henrietta worried anew over school. Would Aunt Tillie really let her go in an old everyday dress? It was worrisome. One of Aunt Tillie's favorite stories was how she wore the same dress from fourth grade through sixth grade just by letting down the hem. "Built character in me," Aunt Tillie always ended it.

The next morning Henrietta stayed in bed quite a while thinking things over. Maybe she should take another look at the Johnson girls' dresses. The green looked bright, she remembered. And she'd never had a green dress.

But when she got downstairs, the dresses were gone. She didn't want to come out and say, "Where're the dresses? I'll take another look at 'em." She wanted Aunt Tillie to say it. She waited all morning for Aunt Tillie to say it. In the afternoon they all piled into the car to go to town, and still Aunt Tillie didn't say it.

A little hope took root that Aunt Tillie was going to buy her a dress, after all. But Henrietta got out of the car with her pail of eggs, and Aunt Tillie didn't say that, either.

Henrietta had never gone to town in an everyday dress. She and Aunt Tillie always put on their best clothes. Even Pa changed his shirt and shoes. She felt stared at. "That must be one of the Strout kids," she imagined everyone thinking.

When she got back from Mrs. Swensen's, she got right in the car. And just in time! She saw Clara, hand in hand with Ruby from their room, coming up the street.

Henrietta got down on the floor. But down there, she worried that Clara would recognize the car and look inside. And once down, she was afraid to come up. There was no telling where Clara and Ruby might be. Supposing they stopped to look in store windows. They'd be right in front of the car when she stuck up her head.

Suddenly the door opened. "Whatcha doin' down there?" came Aunt Tillie's voice.

Henrietta picked herself up. "I don't want nobody seeing my dress," she said, feeling aggrieved and foolish at the same time.

Aunt Tillie had ready-made lectures for remarks like that. But she said nothing.

Going home, Henrietta got so anxious she couldn't sit still. "I don't have nothin' to wear to school," she said at last, hunching up close to Aunt Tillie in the front seat.

Still Aunt Tillie said nothing.

Henrietta flopped to the back of the seat. "What'm I gonna do?" she wailed.

"You got them perfectly nice dresses Emma Johnson brung over! Cut down, the green and purple'll look like they was brand new."

"But it's only three days to school," fretted Henrietta, throwing herself forward again.

"I'll get right at 'em soon as we get home."

Without her sewing machine, Aunt Tillie didn't finish the dresses until the evening before school. "There now," she said, handing them to Henrietta. "I done a good job on 'em if I do say so myself."

Henrietta ran upstairs to Aunt Tillie's mirror to try on the green dress—the purple was out of the question!

Standing on tiptoe she could see the top third of the dress. Getting up on the bed, she saw the middle third. Jumping up and down she caught a few glimpses of the bottom before Aunt Tillie yelled up, "You're gonna break them bedsprings!"

She liked it! She thought it made her look—well, not ordinary. It seemed all at once a magical dress that would do wonderful things for the wearer. It would make her always say just the right thing at the right time. And everybody would say, "How can it be that this popular girl is the same girl who used to be so homespun?"

CHAPTER 4

The dress lost its magic the next day when Henrietta put on her coat to go to school.

"What're you wearing your coat for on a warm day like this?" Aunt Tillie wanted to know.

"So Nellie won't see her dress when I get on the bus."

"Goodness gracious!" scoffed Aunt Tillie. "I never seen such a silly girl! What does it matter if Nellie sees it? She knows you got it! You're gonna roast in that coat!"

That put Henrietta in a bad humor.

Then the bus was late pulling up in front of the schoolhouse. The going-in bell had already rung. Fearful of being late, everyone ran madly for the schoolhouse. Henrietta, in her hot, heavy coat, got left behind. The hall was empty when she got inside.

But a little of opening day excitement returned as she climbed the stairs. Seventh grade was on second floor. It was the only thing different about seventh grade. She would still have only one teacher. She would still have to sit at her desk all day long. Moving from room to room didn't come until high school. All the same, going up the stairs made her feel grown up. She ran up them, nobody being in sight.

But the eighth grade teacher was at the top. "Go back and walk!" she ordered, and stared at Henrietta as if storing her up in her memory for future reference.

That squelched every bit of opening day excitement.

Seventh grade room was so quiet Henrietta thought she was late for sure. Miss Hawes was at the board with her back to the class. But everyone was seated. And nobody was talking.

Then Henrietta remembered that last year's seventh graders had warned, "Watch out! Miss Hawes can see with her back turned!"

Though in a dreadful hurry, Henrietta

didn't toss her coat over a hook. She hung it up carefully—in case Miss Hawes saw through walls, too.

But at the cloakroom doorway, she suddenly stopped. Did her dress look like a woman's dress? It felt very roomy. And six rows of staring eyes were waiting for her to come out.

Last bell rang. Miss Hawes's heels clicked to her desk. "Eunice Anderson," she began the roll call.

Henrietta swished out of the cloakroom, swished past Miss Hawes, swished into the first seat she came to, though it put her right in front of Miss Hawes's desk.

"Henrietta Hanson."

"Present." Henrietta pulled in her dress where it was hanging out in the aisle.

"Hope Harmon."

Ruby's hand went up. "The Harmons have moved. Their farm was foreclosed."

Henrietta looked back at Ruby, who turned out to be sitting next to Clara. What will Ruby do now? she wondered. Last year Ruby and Hope were best friends. Theirs was a paired off room. There was nobody left over for Ruby. Eunice had the only group, and Eunice would never let somebody like Ruby in it. Only the most popular got into Eunice's group.

Remembering she'd seen Ruby and Clara walking hand in hand down Main Street, Henrietta faced front uneasily. Then dismissed her worry. Ruby was less popular than she was. There was no hope for Ruby. Last year the teacher was always saying, "Ruby, if you'd pay more attention to what you're doing, and less attention to what everybody else is doing, you wouldn't get so many F's on your papers."

Roll call over, Miss Hawes put aside the register and said, "I realize you have probably sat next to your best friend. Nevertheless, I'm going to let you keep the seat you've chosen. But if I catch you talking, you'll be moved."

Henrietta was stunned. She didn't *choose* her seat. She just sat in it. She tried to catch Clara's eyes. But Clara was looking at Ruby. The two were exchanging delighted looks.

Again Henrietta faced front uneasily. And again dismissed her worry. Ruby would talk. Ruby talked to everybody, even to the popular kids, who ignored her. Ruby was sure to get moved.

Books were being passed out, and the room was full of thumps. Henrietta's head was deep in her drawer, which she was determined to keep this year so she could find things, when a hush fell over the room. Henrietta took her head out of her drawer and saw that a new girl had come into the room.

The girl's pa, a big burly man with his hat on, brought her in. He took her as far as Miss Hawes's desk, tipped his hat to Miss Hawes, then turned without a word and left.

To Henrietta, it seemed that the new girl had dropped from heaven. Here was somebody for Ruby!

The new girl stood with her head bent over. Not much could be seen of her but a mass of tight, frizzy brown curls. She'll be popular, thought Henrietta, gazing with envy at the curls.

At the sound of the door closing behind her pa, the girl raised her head. She wasn't as pretty as Henrietta expected from such an abundance of curls. Her face was too long and too narrow. Her gray eyes were striking, though. They were unusually large. But they made her thin face look all eyes.

Then the new girl smiled, her smile taking in the whole class. It was too big a smile. It cut her narrow face in two. And there was something else wrong with the smile. It was too eager. It was not the smile of a popular girl.

"So you're from Minneapolis, Vanessa," said Miss Hawes, looking at the little pink card that came with new pupils.

Vanessa took her big smile away from the class and gave it to Miss Hawes. "No ma'am. We was in Minneapolis when the carnival went broke."

The class tittered. Kids in Prairie Springs didn't call teachers "ma'am."

Miss Hawes looked up severely. The tittering stopped.

"What brought your family to Prairie Springs, Vanessa?" Miss Hawes asked. "Do you have relatives here?"

"No ma'am, we got—"

A lone titter broke out, seemed out of control, but stopped abruptly when Miss Hawes's severe eye found it.

"We got Aunt Belle; you know, Belle's Beauty Parlor," went on Vanessa eagerly, as if she had no suspicion the titters were at her. "But she ain't no relation. I call her Aunt Belle cuz Ma told me to. Her and Ma was best friends before Ma and Pa got hitched. Ma wrote we was stuck in Minneapolis and could she give her a job. And Aunt Belle wrote back, 'Come on.' Pa ain't got a job yet. But he's looking. He wants us to stay put here." The last sentence was directed at the class, along with the eager smile.

Henrietta looked away. Vanessa's eager smile in the face of the titters was unbearable.

There's an empty seat in row five, Vanessa," said Miss Hawes. "You can sit there."

"Yes, ma'am."

Miss Hawes's eyes swept the room fiercely. Not a titter to be heard!

Vanessa took her seat, and the passing out of books was resumed.

At morning recess, Clara's and Ruby's row was dismissed before Henrietta's. They got ahead of her in line. Out on the playground she had to run to catch up with them. She saw that Ruby had one of Clara's hands. So she took the other.

"I was in a cyclone!" Henrietta burst out with it right away.

Ruby gave Clara a meaningful look. "I told you I bet she was going to be just like her auntie about it."

Henrietta didn't understand what Ruby was talking about. She went on. "We was that close to it!" She held up a thumb and forefinger to show a hair's breath. "But the cyclone didn't touch nobody. Aunt Tillie stood at the—"

"We know! We know!" broke in Clara. "Everybody knows! Everybody's heard it again and again!"

"A hundred times!" echoed Ruby.

Henrietta stared at them in bewilderment.

"Last Saturday afternoon in every store your

Aunt Tillie went into, she told about that cyclone," explained Clara. "It didn't matter if she knew you or not. She saw somebody, she went right up to them and said. 'I was in a cyclone!' Ma says before she left town she knew that cyclone by heart."

"My ma says it was coming out her ears," chimed in Ruby.

Henrietta was mortified. So that was why Aunt Tillie had been in such a hurry to get to town. Pacing the floor while Pa washed up.

"I was in my sister's wedding," said Ruby, taking over. "And guess what? I caught the bouquet. Ain't that funny! Me the next to get married!"

Clara laughed. Henrietta laughed, too. But her laugh sounded raucous in her ears, rather like a crow's caw. She couldn't get over her mortification. There were times when Aunt Tillie talked too much. And always the worst times. Always away from home where people stared. Am I getting like her? Henrietta worried. She kept her mouth shut the rest of the recess period.

They were a threesome again at the lunch table, with Clara in the middle. The table conversation was about Vanessa.

"At recess you know what that new girl Vanessa did?" said the girl across the table. "She went up to Eunice's group and asked, 'Can I go around with you guys?' "

Clara's eyes widened. "That's the nerviest thing I ever heard of!"

"I think carnival people are like that," suggested Ruby. "You know, they don't stay nowhere, so they're pushy."

"I'm going to stay away from her," said the girl across the table.

"Me, too," went up and down the table.

Henrietta, her head bent over her sandwich, said nothing. She was thinking that school was more taxing than she'd remembered. It was a struggle just to keep your place. And there seemed no end to these girls you must stay away from. Last year Ida. Now Vanessa. It wore her out.

There being nothing more to be said about Vanessa, Ruby went back to her sister's wedding. "I was a bridesmaid in my sister's wedding," she said loudly enough for the whole room to hear. "And you know what? I was the youngest bridesmaid anybody ever saw. Everybody said so."

When the farm girls lined up to go out for noon recess, Henrietta whispered to Clara, "Don't it drive you crazy the way Ruby don't stop talking about her sister's wedding."

Clara widened her eyes and said nothing.

On the playground, Clara pulled her hand away when Henrietta tried to take it. Henrietta felt she was being punished for saying something mean about Ruby. She would have said something nice about Ruby to make up for the mean thing, if she could have thought of anything nice.

Ruby and Clara held hands. Henrietta stuck her own hands in her pockets to hide their lonesomeness. Unattached that way, she lost the two girls whenever they made sudden turns. She had to run to catch up.

They had just made a sudden turn, and Henrietta had just caught up, when suddenly Vanessa was facing them. "Can I go around with you guys?" she asked, her smile eager.

Clara's eyes grew very wide, "You can't *ask!* You got to *be* asked!"

But Vanessa just kept smiling as if she didn't understand.

Ruby glanced slyly at Henrietta. "Why don't you ask Henrietta," she said, "She—"

"Me and Clara's best friends!" cut in Henrietta loudly, too loudly. And she grabbed Clara's hand. To Henrietta's horror, Clara tried to shake her hand loose. Henrietta hung on.

The bell rang. Clara and Ruby broke away at a run. Henrietta also ran, ran for dear life. She ended up near the head of the line. She didn't dare look around for Clara and Ruby. She was afraid her eyes might land on Vanessa, smiling eagerly.

When she got home from school, Henrietta felt too beaten to go into the house where Aunt Tillie would be waiting with questions. She put her books down by the pump and sat down beside them, resting her chin in her hands.

How dirty the barnyard looked with its clutter: the broken hay wagon, the worn-out tires, the useless ladder with two steps missing, the heap of debris from the cyclone—and the smell of manure! When she stayed home all day, she didn't notice the smell. But after being away, she felt suffocated by it.

"Ain'tcha coming in?" Aunt Tillie called from the doorway.

So Henrietta picked up her books and went inside.

"Was your friends glad to see you?" was Aunt Tillie's first question.

Henrietta wearily dropped her books onto the table. "I guess so."

"What'd you mean 'guess so'? I bet Clara was tickled pink to see you. Didcha tell 'em you was in a cyclone?"

"Sh-sh!" said Henrietta, sitting down and picking up a pencil. "I gotta do an arithmetic problem."

"Count five days to the week. Take away twenty days for holidays," she mumbled. "That comes to one hundred and sixty!" She dropped the pencil in exhaustion. How could she possibly get through one hundred sixty days of school if all one hundred sixty of them were like today?

"That your school work you doin'?" asked Aunt Tillie, looking over Henrietta's shoulder.

"Sort of." Henrietta wearily opened her arithmetic book to the chapter on the metric system. She didn't understand it. She hadn't understood it last year in sixth grade. What did it matter that the French used meters. France was across the ocean.

Wearily Henrietta read the first problem. "Suppose a car holds 5 qts. of oil. Is 5 liters of oil too much or too little to fill the car?"

Who cared?

She read the second problem. "Which should you be able to run more quickly, a 100-meter dash or a 100-yard dash?"

Now that was more interesting. At the Fourth of July celebration last summer she won a prize, five free ice cream cones, for coming in first in the girls' 100-yard dash. She glanced up at the chart and saw that a meter was 3.37 inches longer than a yard.

"Which would you rather have?" she read aloud to Aunt Tillie, still hanging over her shoulder. "A liter of milk or a quart of milk?"

Aunt Tillie backed off. "You do your lessons," she said. "I got ironing to do."

As meters turned into millimeters, and grams into kilograms, Henrietta's weariness slid away. A quietness came over her. The day began to seem not so bad. After all, it was the first day. And firsts were always a bit of a strain. In bed that night she fell asleep wondering if some day she would sail across the ocean and sit in a French restaurant and have a hectogram of cake and a half liter of coffee with a deciliter of cream to put in it and a centigram of sugar to sweeten it.

In the morning, Henrietta was ready for a new start. What went wrong yesterday, she figured out as she dressed, was that she was afraid Ruby was trying to cut her out. So she tried to cut Ruby out.

The thing to do, she decided on the way to the bus stop, was to be a group—like Eunice's. To be sure, Eunice's group really had two pairs in it. Eunice and Margy were best friends. And so were Amy and Beth. Yet back in fourth grade there'd been five in Eunice's group. If five worked, why not three?

In arithmetic something wonderful happened. Henrietta got a hundred in the test on the metric system. She never got hundreds in arithmetic. She always made goofy mistakes, things she knew better than to do. But when she lifted a corner of her paper to peek (Miss Hawes always returned papers face down), there it was. One hundred.

The glow of the hundred still lingered with Henrietta when she went out to morning recess. She felt up to *anything*.

But before she could mention the "group," Ruby said, "Eunice says you're wearing a woman's dress. She says only women wear low V-necks like yours. And I guess Eunice ought to know, seeing as how her ma runs a dress shop."

"Your neck's so low your slip shows," pointed out Clara. "Didn't you notice *that?*"

Henrietta stared down in shame at the offending slip. She couldn't understand how she had missed noticing. Or how Aunt Tillie had missed. Even Pa should've noticed *that*. The rest of the day Henrietta was too occupied keeping her hands over where her slip showed to bring up the "group."

The next day Henrietta wore the purple with the zigzagging stripes while Aunt Tillie sewed up the V-neck.

"Only old people wear purple," Ruby said with a sniff at morning recess.

"Is that one of the Johnson girls' dresses?" asked Clara.

Henrietta looked at her in alarm.

"Last night I told Ma about your low neck," explained Clara. "And Ma said it must of been one of the dresses Mrs. Johnson gave you of her girls' things."

So everybody knew! Henrietta's face felt hot with shame.

"Their things was all just old stuff." She tried to shrug it off. "Nothin' fit."

Clara's eyes widened. "That's not nice when somebody gives you something."

"We gave a lot of our old stuff to the Harmons when all their things was auctioned off," reproached Ruby, "and they said, 'Thank you.' "

Henrietta feld doomed. She felt she was never going to learn to say the right thing. She didn't mention the "group." She was afraid it might turn out to be a dumb idea.

But at noon recess—without Henrietta mentioning it—they became the hoped-for group.

This was brought about by Eunice's announcement of her birthday party.

"The Saturday after this coming Saturday is my twelfth birthday," Eunice told the seventh grade girls gathering around her. "My mother says I can have any kind of party I want and invite as many as I want. So I'm having it at the country club, and I'm inviting almost the whole room."

That brought forth little squeals of delight. Even Vanessa, who had pushed her way up to the front, let out a whoop, as if she expected to be invited, too.

"First we'll have punch and cookies and stand around and talk like the grownups do," Eunice continued. "Then there's to be a fiddler and a caller who's going to teach us to square dance."

None of them—not Clara, nor Ruby, nor Henrietta—it turned out, had been inside the country club. Nor had any of them danced. They huddled together. "Let's plan it so we get there at at exactly the same time so we can go in together," said Clara. "Let's stick together inside, too," said Ruby.

The very next morning Eunice started giving out invitations. She passed them out in the room before school. She could only do a few,

Eunice explained, because of homework. But she'd do the rest over the weekend, she promised, and bring them Monday morning.

Henrietta watched with envy as Eunice went up and down the aisles handing big white envelopes to the "chosen." Only the most popular got them. Roland DeRuyter got one.

Without much to do out on the farm, Henrietta had lots of time over the weekend to think about Eunice's party. Sometimes she thought it was going to be the "most fun ever." Other times she panicked. What if she couldn't learn square dancing? Was clumsy. And everybody laughed.

When Aunt Tillie stepped out to get some clothes off the line, Henrietta went skipping about the kitchen, clapping her hands and twirling, which is what Clara, who'd seen square dancing, said they did.

"What's goin' on in here?" asked Aunt Tillie, stepping back in sooner than expected.

"Nothin'." Henrietta didn't want to tell about the party. Not just yet. Not 'til she got her invitation.

Not that she was worried about getting an invitation. Hadn't Eunice said she was inviting *everybody?* Well, almost everybody. But it was understood that the "almost" was put in to keep Vanessa out.

Yet in bed Sunday night, with Monday morning going to be there when she woke up, Henrietta got the shivers—or shakes, or something—so badly her teeth chattered. And she felt a little glad that exciting things like Eunice's party didn't happen just every day.

Eunice brought the rest of the invitations to school Monday morning. She carried them in a shoebox.

But when she started up an aisle with her box, Miss Hawes frowned and said, "We don't permit the passing out of invitations to outside activities in the classroom."

Eunice's face got very red. She sat down. The box went under her seat.

The box didn't come out until the school day was over. Eunice stood just outside the schoolyard giving away invitations. Some kids, not wanting to appear anxious, hurried past. Eunice had to call them back. Others, Henrietta among them, hovered close by, waiting to be named. Henrietta waited until she heard the roar of the buses as they prepared to pull off. That sent her flying.

When Henrietta sat down in the bus, she felt a little queasy. Sort of like being sick at her stomach.

Then, as the bus jiggled and rattled toward

home, she cheered up—a little bit, anyway. It had to be that Eunice didn't see her.

After all, she always got a valentine from Eunice, though Eunice usually forgot someone. Last year she forgot Ruby. Yet Ruby got an invitation.

Of course, there was the mean thing Eunice said about the V-neck. But goodness, that didn't mean nothin'. Eunice was just naturally snippy about clothes, what with her ma owning a dress shop.

But when all of Tuesday morning went by and she still didn't get an invitation, Henrietta lost hope. She felt she'd die of shame if anybody found out.

So for the life of her, Henrietta couldn't understand why, when at the lunch table Clara asked her, "What're you wearing to Eunice's party?" she answered, "I didn't get an invitation."

Clara and Ruby were astonished. They couldn't understand it.

Out on the playground Clara and Ruby still couldn't understand it. "I'll ask Eunice why she left you out," volunteered Ruby.

"No!" shouted Henrietta, though she didn't mean to shout. But it was getting unbearable, the way Clara and Ruby couldn't understand it.

The minute Eunice was back from lunch at home, Ruby was over talking to her. Right away Ruby was back to report, "Eunice says she didn't invite you because she wants everybody to look especially nice at her party, and she don't think you got a party dress to wear."

"I got a party dress," said Henrietta, her cheeks on fire.

"One of the Johnson girls' dresses?" asked Ruby. The expression on Ruby's face was not nice as she said it. Nor was the expression on Clara's face nice as she listened.

"It's store-bought!" answered Henrietta rashly.

"Where? A rummage sale?"

"Anderson's Dress Shop!" Right away Henrietta knew she'd said a dumb thing. Ruby could find out. All Ruby had to do was ask Eunice.

"I'm gonna ask Eunice to ask her ma if you got a dress there!" said Ruby.

"Go ahead!" Henrietta braved it out.

The ringing of the bell saved Henrietta for the time being. But she felt her fibbing had undone her. Eunice would go home and ask her mother, "Did Henrietta's aunt come in the store and buy a dress?" And Mrs. Anderson would answer, "You mean that farm woman who's fat as a pig and goes around looking at every price tag, and asking in her loud voice, 'Is this price right? Is this price right?' No! Thank goodness!"

That night in bed, after a good deal of tossing and turning—the old iron springs rasping and twanging—Henrietta concluded that the only way out was to stay home the rest of the week. By Monday, the party over, it would be safe to go back. The trouble was, Aunt Tillie, who'd quit school at sixth grade and wished she hadn't, didn't believe in missing school, and didn't believe in headaches and stomachaches on school mornings, either.

Henrietta tossed and turned some more, but couldn't figure out what to do. If only something would happen! Anything at all! Well, not a cyclone. But something!

CHAPTER 5

Henrietta woke with a start. She felt something had frightened her awake. She lay very still, looking about from side to side out of the corner of her eyes. Nothing moved in the darkness.

Pa's thunderous snores rolled out of his room, and from across the hall came the little whistle Aunt Tillie made as she breathed in and out. They were comforting sounds. They seemed to say, "We're here, so go back to sleep."

Outdoors, though, the wind was on a rampage. It shook the windows across the hall as if it wanted to rip them off. When she was little, Henrietta believed the wind rattled the windows at night because it wanted to get in out of the dark. She'd felt a compulsion, back then, to open a window and let it in.

She had half a mind to open a window now. The house needed the wind to come rushing through it, cleaning it out. There was something the matter with the air in her room. It choked her up, like the air in the hayloft when she swung by a rope and dropped into the dry, dusty hay.

Why, the air was full of dust!

Across the hall Aunt Tillie's bed gave a great lurch, followed by a heavy thump. Aunt Tillie was up! It must be morning. Henrietta hopped out of bed and pattered into Aunt Tillie's room, which was almost as dark as the closet. "The air's full of dust," she said.

"A dust storm's blowing outdoors," said Aunt Tillie, sounding funny with no teeth.

"Maybe there won't be school."

"A little dust ain't gonna shut nothin' down," scoffed Aunt Tillie.

Henrietta pattered back to bed.

On the way downstairs, Aunt Tillie stopped at Henrietta's door. "Whatcha go back to bed for? You'll need to get out to the bus early in this wind."

Henrietta got reluctantly out of bed. What

if she missed the bus, didn't see it in the dust. No, that wouldn't work. Pa would take her in their old Model T Ford when he finished milking. She'd get there in the middle of geography. Miss Hawes would frown and say, "Why is it, Henrietta, you are the *only* one who didn't see the bus?"

Dressing was slow. She had to shake the dust out of everything. It got into her eyes, and she had to rub them. It got into her mouth, and she had to cough it out.

"You better get on down here!" came Aunt Tillie's call from the foot of the stairs. "It's nearly bus time!"

"Coming!" One stocking had a hole in the toe. The hole was just big enough to let her big toe through uncomfortably.

"You don't get down here, you ain't gonna have time to eat!"

"Coming!" Henrietta pushed her big toe back inside the stocking and stepped into her shoes. She tied the strings with a jerk that broke one of them.

"Henrietta Hanson!"

"Coming!" She went clattering down the stairs. Halfway down she felt the big toe working its way uncomfortably out again.

The lamp was lit. Aunt Tillie was busy trying to keep the dust out. With a blunt knife, she was poking rags into the cracks around the window frames.

Henrietta went to a window and looked out. At times she could barely make out the barn. "Where's the dust coming from?" she asked.

"From our fields!" answered Aunt Tillie bitterly. "It's blowing all the topsoil off."

Henrietta understood the seriousness of that. Under the topsoil was clay, and everybody knew you couldn't grow anything in clay.

"You ain't got time for looking out windows," said Aunt Tillie. "I got your oatmeal dished. You eat. I'll watch for the bus."

The oatmeal had already been sugared, Henrietta noticed. Aunt Tillie didn't trust her with the sugar bowl now that they didn't have money to buy sugar. There was a film of dust on the cream in the pitcher. She pushed the dust back with a spoon, but the cream that poured out looked gray.

"I can't tell one set of car lights from another. You better get on out there and wait at the mailbox," fretted Aunt Tillie.

"It's too dusty to wait out there."

"Here it comes!"

Henrietta sprang from the table, upsetting her chair. She stooped to pick it up.

"Let it be! Let it be! I'll get it!" Aunt Tillie's carpet came slapping across the floor.

Henrietta shoved her arms into her coat sleeves, grabbed up books and lunch bag, and dashed for the door. A pail got in the way and went rattling across the room. Pa's mackinaw dropped off the hook and had to be kicked aside. None of this slowed Henrietta. She was out of the door before Aunt Tillie had straightened the chair.

The wind nearly knocked her over. She saw Pa coming out of the barn with the milk pails, walking at a near run to get the milk inside out of the dust. She didn't stop to wave at him. She plowed into the wind.

"You forgot your cap! You'll get an earache in this wind!" Aunt Tillie was out on the step flapping Henrietta's cap in the air, holding onto it with both hands to keep the wind from taking it away.

Henrietta ran back, grabbed the cap from Aunt Tillie's outstretched hands, stuffed it into her pocket, and was off.

"Your ears ain't in your pocket!" followed after her.

Without slowing, Henrietta got the cap out of her pocket with one hand and over her head. But before she could secure it, the wind snatched it off. For a moment she stood watching as the cap whirled off in a cloud of dust. Then she ran on.

She felt a shoe loosen and glanced down. The broken lace had come undone. No time to fix it.

The bus was gaining on her. The very wind that was holding her back seemed to be pushing the bus forward. She put on a burst of speed. And off flew the shoe. It went skittering into the ditch along the highway—with Henrietta hot in pursuit.

She was away from the wind down in the ditch. But the high, brittle weeds shook off dust into her face as she moved among them. And when she found the shoe, the lace was missing. Up above, the kids in the bus were banging on the windows for her to hurry. Hanging onto the weeds, she pulled herself up the embankment. When she tried to step up into the bus, the shoe dropped off her foot. She had to pick it up and carry it on.

The din inside the bus was deafening. At first Henrietta thought the yelling was at her. Then she saw that all eyes were turned toward the back where two boys were fighting. The bus driver was half-turned in his seat, bellowing, "Quiet down back there!"

The fighting had emptied the seats in the back and filled up the rest of the bus. There was no place to sit except at the back. Well, there was an empty seat halfway down. But Roland DeRuyter had his legs propped across it so nobody could sit in it.

In her quandary, Henrietta didn't hear the shifting of gears behind her. When the bus lurched forward, she went sprawling to the floor, books flying, only the lost shoe remaining firmly implanted under her arm.

A girl seated nearby gathered up Henrietta's books. Together they looked for the lunch bag, but couldn't find it. When Henrietta stood up, she saw she'd been sitting on it. It was squashed flat. The paper was purple with jelly squeezed out of the sandwiches.

Holding the bag far out in front so the stickiness wouldn't touch her coat, Henrietta proceeded down the aisle.

When she came to the seat beside Roland, she saw that he had removed his legs. So she sat down, taking care not to look at him, lest he tell her to move on.

Two very dirty toes were now sticking out of her stocking. But she didn't know how to go about getting her shoe on. It was wedged tightly under her arm. One of her hands was full of books. The other held the lunch bag. There was no place to put anything, except a little space between them on the seat. She took a quick look at Roland, staring out the window. So she set the bag on the seat, then quickly bent over and put on the shoe.

As she straightened, Henrietta glanced at Roland to make sure he wasn't looking. She thought she saw a motion—a breeze, almost—as if his head had moved suddenly, but it was turned toward the window.

She left the lunch bag on the seat. Holding it out in front of her was tiresome.

Outside, the black wind seemed at times to be trying to lift the bus right off the highway. But the big old bus lumbered on, unworried.

Inside the air was hazy with dust, making everyone appear to be at a distance, making even the trouble over the dress seem far away. The dust storm will keep us in, she thought. Ruby won't get a chance to talk to Eunice.

The bus jogged. Voices rose and fell. A feeling of well-being crept over Henrietta. She felt friendly toward everybody. Even toward the fighting boys at the back. Even toward Roland at her side. Though she wished he wouldn't keep his back turned. But then, he didn't like anybody.

Except Miss Hawes! Henrietta knew Roland liked Miss Hawes because once in the recess line a boy, mimicking the way Miss Hawes clipped off her words, said, "*We* will have it quiet in this line!"

Roland said, "Cut it out."

And the boy didn't do it again.

It was strange that Miss Hawes should be the one person in the room Roland liked. Miss Hawes didn't laugh or joke or have fun with the class. She just taught. And she had two deep lines between her eyes and around her mouth that made her look as though she were always frowning.

Miss Hawes was fair, though. Henrietta gave her credit for that. She treated the dumb kids the same as the smart kids. And when she explained something to a dumb kid, and the dumb kid still couldn't learn it, she didn't get cross. She acted as if she understood exactly how it felt not to be able to learn it. Was that why Roland liked Miss Hawes?

Henrietta could control her curiosity no longer. She looked right at Roland. It seemed a safe thing to do. He was still staring out the window.

How clean and neat he was. His hair was

as straight as if he'd just run a comb through it. She'd forgotten to comb her hair, Henrietta remembered. It was just as well. After the wind got through with it, the combing would have been all for nothing.

And his shirt looked as if it'd just come off the ironing board. Not a wrinkle or spot on it. She noticed some yellow spots on the front of her dress. Last night's fried eggs, she decided. She wet a thumb and rubbed at the spots. But the yellow stayed. And a black smudge was added.

Eunice said Roland was a spiffy dresser. But Henrietta thought it was just that he looked so perfectly neat—like his school papers, which were always getting put up on the bulletin board. Her own never got up there. Too many crossed-out words. She felt all at once utterly, hopelessly messy. She looked away from Roland, looked out the window across the aisle.

"One, two, three, four," she counted as the fence posts flew by. Sometimes she had to count fence posts. She didn't know why. She just had to. Once when she missed the bus and had to walk home, she counted every single post. It came to nine hundred and twenty-three posts.

But these posts were jumping by too fast. They made her head ache. She closed her eyes, and not until she felt the bus slowing to a stop did she open them. The bus was pulling up in front of the schoolhouse.

At once the stampede for the door was on. Henrietta would have just as soon waited. But she thought Roland might want to get out. So she hoisted the books under her arm, picked up the lunch bag, which felt squishy, got to her feet, and took a step toward the clogged aisle.

"Look what you done!" exploded behind her. Roland was staring in outrage at a purple spot on his tan jacket, the side that'd been next to her lunch bag. "You ruined my new jacket!"

It was only a little spot! Henrietta tried to get into the aisle. Nobody would let her in.

She heard, or maybe felt—the clamor in the bus was deafening—a little plop. She looked down and saw that a sandwich had broken through the bag. There was another little plop as a squashed hard boiled egg joined the sandwich.

From behind came a short laugh, an angry laugh still smarting with outrage.

That was mean, laughing because she'd lost her lunch! Henrietta felt tears stinging her eyes. She blinked to hold them back.

There was another laugh, not such an angry laugh this time, sounding loud and clear in the suddenly nearly empty bus. "Holy cow! You've sat on the darn thing!"

Henrietta twisted her neck to look over her shoulder. She saw a big purple spot on the back of her brown coat. She could just hear Aunt Tillie saying, "There ain't no money to buy a new one. You'll just have to make do with a purple-spotted coat!"

Holding the lunch bag upside down to save the remaining sandwich, she marched up the aisle with as much dignity as she could muster. But when she stepped down from the bus, the shoe dropped off. And when she stooped to put it back on, the bag righted itself, and the last sandwich dropped out. A tear rolled down her cheek. Before she could brush it off, she felt the ground jar under Roland's jump. She quickly turned her head away.

"Here," he said. "Use this."

Henrietta kept her head turned.

A piece of twine dropped at her feet. She got down on a knee and strung her shoe with it. When she looked up, Roland was going into the schoolhouse.

She let the wind have the empty bag. It went flapping down the street like a purple spotted chicken running for its life.

Suddenly she realized she was all alone.

Everybody had gone in out of the dust. She could run home. Nobody would see her. She hesitated. The going-in bell rang. She obediently ran to the schoolhouse.

It was during arithmetic, with recess coming up next, that Henrietta noticed the quiet. Almost no wind! Her ears strained for the sound of it. But with each tick of the clock, the world outside the window grew quieter.

Recess bell rang. Miss Hawes went to the window and looked out. Henrietta held her breath. "We'll go out," was the verdict.

In the cloakroom Henrietta stayed at her hook and pretended to be looking for something in her coat pockets, digging around in them until everybody was out. She was the last to get in line. When the line moved out of the building, she dropped off and stood in a corner of the entryway.

The day was still dark. Dust hung in the air as if it didn't want to come down to the schoolyard. Nobody will see me here, thought Henrietta, and faced the wall, the better not to be seen.

But pretty soon she turned to find out what was going on. Clara and Ruby were strolling back and forth, chattering away, not missing her at all. She returned to the wall.

But her eyes would go back. This time Ruby

was with Eunice. So now Eunice knew about the dress! Henrietta faced the wall for good.

Suddenly someone was breathing on the back of her neck. Henrietta wheeled around. Vanessa was so close, their noses bumped.

"How about you and me being best friends?" Vanessa smiled.

Up close like this, Vanessa's smile looked enormous. Henrietta jerked a thumb toward Clara, who was now walking arm in arm with Ruby. "Me and Clara are best friends," she said, her eyes defying Vanessa to disbelieve.

Vanessa didn't bat an eyelash. "You want a second-best friend?"

Henrietta saw that Eunice was now looking straight at the corner where she stood. So she let Vanessa lead her down the steps. Then Henrietta took over, steering them far away from the schoolhouse.

"I been to lots of schools. I bet I been to a school in every state there is. I bet there ain't nobody been to as many schools as me," chattered Vanessa happily, swinging the hand that held Henrietta's.

"I've only been here," admitted Henrietta, noticing over her shoulder that Eunice and Ruby were together again, hatching up goodness only knows what!

"You're lucky. It ain't so hot going from school to school. Pa wants us to stay put. He says a carnival ain't no place for a kid. I was in seventh grade last year. But the last seventh grade teacher—I bet I had more seventh grade teachers than you seen in your lifetime—well, heck, that old teacher wouldn't pass me. But don'tcha tell nobody!"

"I won't," promised Henrietta.

"You was the first girl I noticed when I was standing up in front of the room. But I didn't know then you was gonna be my second-best friend. I'd of been jumping up and down for joy if I'd of known."

"You only noticed me because I sat right in front of you," said Henrietta coldly. She didn't want Vanessa to get the idea that just because she was walking with her now, she was going to do it *every* day. I'll say "Hi" to her, she thought, and I'll smile at her. But that's all.

"No, it wasn't that," said Vanessa, still smiling, seeming not to have noticed the coldness in Henrietta's voice. "You was different from the others. You got nice eyes."

There it was again. "Nice." "I don't know what 'nice' eyes mean," said Henrietta.

"Nice eyes is when you look at somebody,

and that person's eyes say to you, 'You don't need to be scairt of me. I'll be nice to you.' "

Henrietta quickly turned her eyes away lest Vanessa see in them something to change her mind. She couldn't recall being nice to anybody. Not mean. But not nice. How could she when it took all she could do just to look out for herself?

"That Clara character says you can't ask. She says you gotta *be* asked. But what if nobody asks you? What're you supposed to do then?" asked Vanessa unexpectedly.

There was something in Vanessa's voice that made Henrietta glance at her sharply. But Vanessa was still smiling.

The bell caught them on the far side of the yard. By running they caught up with the line as it moved into the building.

The rest of the morning, Vanessa kept getting into Henrietta's thoughts. Vanessa was easy to talk to . . . Vanessa understood more than she let on . . . Vanessa's smile didn't get on your nerves after you were around her awhile. You got used to it.

In the cafeteria the girl across the table had a juicy tidbit to tell on Vanessa. "That new girl Vanessa went up to Eunice, and you know what she did? She said, 'You forgot to give me an invitation.' " The girl looked at Henrietta as she said it.

Clara was shocked. She looked wide-eyed at Henrietta. "That's the pushiest thing I ever heard of!"

Henrietta, without a sandwich to busy herself with, didn't know where to put her eyes.

"Eunice told her off," said the girl across the table, "Eunice said, 'I didn't invite you to my party because I *don't want* you at my party!' "

"You gotta tell pushy kids off," said Clara (to Henrietta). "It's the only way you can get rid of them."

I mustn't have anything to do with Vanessa anymore, decided Henrietta. I mustn't even smile at her.

Ruby leaned across Clara. "Hey, Henrietta! I told Eunice what you said about buying a dress at her ma's store."

"I remember I didn't get it there. I remember I got it somewhere else."

"Eunice says she can't wait to see it at her party."

"I'm not going. I wasn't invited."

Ruby's hand came up from her lap with a large white envelope in it. "Eunice found your invitation. See, it's got your name on it."

It was the longed-for envelope, but Henrietta took it from Ruby as if she were being handed a spider.

When they went out for noon recess, Vanessa was waiting on the steps. Town kids never got back this early! Henrietta was caught by surprise.

"I run all the way," explained Vanessa, taking Henrietta's hand in the confident manner of a best—that is, second-best—friend.

"Your house must be nearby," said Henrietta, too surprised to withdraw her hand.

"Oh, we ain't got a house yet. Aunt Belle's putting us up 'til we get one," said Vanessa, leading Henrietta off.

"Your Aunt Belle's house must be nearby," said Henrietta, too surprised not to be led along.

"You know somebody can get my pa a job?" asked Vanessa worriedly, her narrow face looking very long without its smile. "He needs one terrible. Aunt Belle's acting like she wants us out of her house. Ma says she can't understand it. She says when she and Aunt Belle was beauty operators together, they shared everything, even clothes."

"Nobody's got money to hire nobody these days," said Henrietta, repeating grownups' talk.

"Pa says he'd do anything. He says he'd dig ditches. You know somebody wants a ditch dug?"

Henrietta tried hard to think of someone, but couldn't.

"You know somebody wants something moved? In the carnival, anybody wanted something moved, they called on Pa. You oughta see his muscles. I'll get him to bulge 'em for you sometime."

"What'd your pa do in the carnival?" It was a question Henrietta had been wanting to ask from the first.

"He used to be the strong man. But the locals kept putting up somebody stronger. So he had to give that up. Then he ran a hit the bottle game. You know, you throw balls at bottles, and if you knock over all the bottles you get a Kewpie doll."

"I know!" said Henrietta excitedly. "I found a dime on the sidewalk, and I'm saving it for county fair! I've been practicing. I'm going to win a Kewpie doll!"

Vanessa looked alarmed. "You'll lose your dime! You can't win unless the man who runs it lets you. He only lets big spenders. Heck, he ain't gonna let a little girl."

Henrietta was shocked. For a moment neither spoke. Then Henrietta said gratefully, "It was nice of you to tell me." She got her hand squeezed.

"I betcha you thought it was funny, my pa bringing me into seventh grade like I was a little first grader," said Vanessa unexpectedly.

Henrietta shook her head no. Though, now that Vanessa mentioned it, it did seem funny.

"That's cuz when I start a new school, I don't go. I run off somewhere and hang around all day."

Henrietta was a little shocked, but a little admiring, too. She, herself, would never dare do that.

"We was late my first day here cuz I run out of the house before Pa could bring me. But he caught me right off. There ain't no place to hide in a little jerkwater town like this."

Henrietta could think of some good places, but she thought it best not to tell Vanessa.

"What's that?" asked Vanessa, catching sight of the envelope sticking out of Henrietta's pocket.

Reminded of the fix she was in, Henrietta took the envelope out of her pocket, glanced at it, and put it back. "The invitation to Eunice's party," she said distractedly.

Vanessa gave her curly head a toss. "Heck, who cares." A pause. Then heatedly, "That Eunice character's a snob." Another pause. Then, wistfully, "I didn't get one."

Henrietta said nothing. She was wondering which was worse—not to be invited, or to be invited without a dress to wear.

Vanessa gave her curls another toss. "I been to lots of dances. I bet I been to more than anybody in this jerkwater town."

Again Henrietta said nothing. She was noticing that Vanessa's mouth looked like Roland's when she wasn't smiling. Not turned down at the corners like his. But tight and unhappy like his.

"How many dances you been to?" Vanessa kept on about it.

"None," Henrietta admitted.

Vanessa was suddenly all smile again. "I go with Ma and Pa when they go dancing. Ma likes dancing better'n anything. You should see the way she dolls up when she goes dancing."

"Does your ma have a pretty party dress?" asked Henrietta wistfully.

"Yeah. It's a beaut!"

"Do you have a pretty party dress?"

The smile vanished. "Course I got one! You don't think my ma'd doll herself all up and let me go looking like a ragamuffin, do you?"

Henrietta was apologetic. She hadn't meant that.

Vanessa was apologetic. She hadn't meant that Henrietta meant that.

The two girls walked on, but silently now, each busy with her own thoughts.

"I wish we was sisters!" Vanessa suddenly burst out. "Then if we moved, you'd have to come with us."

That startled Henrietta.

"Hey! We could pass for twins, I betcha!"

Here was a turn that fell in with Henrietta's line of thought. "We're nearly the same size," she said.

Vanessa gave her head a delighted scratch. "Yeah! I tell you what! You let my ma give you a permanent at Belle's like mine, and we wear the same clothes, and we can have a barrel of fun foolin' folks."

"Can I wear your pretty party dress to Eunice's party Saturday night?" Henrietta blurted out. "I don't have one."

Vanessa's face looked as if a damp sponge had passed over it.

But Henrietta persisted. "Please! I'll give it right back. I won't even stay more'n a couple minutes at the party if you don't want me to."

Still Vanessa said nothing. The bell rang. They dropped hands and ran for the line. All at once at odds, they didn't say a word to each other as the line moved into the building.

All afternoon Henrietta's mind strayed from

her lessons to Vanessa's refusal. If Vanessa were a true friend, as she pretended, she'd not turn her back on a friend when that friend was in a pickle. Henrietta's thoughts grew angrier and angrier.

After school, as Henrietta was about to step into the waiting bus, somebody took hold of her elbow. It was Vanessa.

"We're still friends, ain't we?" asked Vanessa.

"Friends share. If you won't let me wear your party dress for even a couple minutes, you can't be my friend," said Henrietta doggedly.

Vanessa's eyes blazed. "To hell with you!"

Henrietta drew back in astonishment and stepped on a foot, which turned out to belong to Roland DeRuyter, who said, "Watch it!" She scarcely noticed him. Her attention was on Vanessa, who was running against those running to catch the busses. Vanessa's elbows were flying, cutting a path through the onrushing bodies.

Who would have guessed Vanessa had such a spiteful side? And with such a big smile, too! All the way home in the bus, Henrietta brooded over Vanessa's spitefulness. She'd better watch out around Vanessa!

But as she ran up the dirt road to her house, Henrietta's anger disappeared. Maybe Vanessa's ma wouldn't let her lend it, she thought. Vanessa hadn't said so because she didn't want to let on that her ma was cross. Henrietta wished she hadn't begged. Just asked, and let it go at that!

But in bed at night, she got angry all over again. She didn't think it was Vanessa's ma, who once upon a time had shared clothes with Aunt Belle. It was Vanessa. And the party was only two nights away! Well, she wouldn't go! But everybody would know why she didn't go. She was in great trouble, and Vanessa could help. But Vanessa wouldn't help. Vanessa was, indeed, a *second-best* friend!

CHAPTER 6

The school morning had scarcely begun when Vanessa came to the front to sharpen her pencil. On the way she dropped a small wad of paper at Henrietta's feet. That was dangerous! Miss Hawes had taught seventh grade too many years not to know that a wad of paper dropped by one girl beside another girl's desk was a note.

Henrietta didn't dare pick up the wad until the morning was half gone. When she did, she was glad Vanessa had taken such a risk. It was a message that wouldn't bear waiting. It read:

"You can have my dress for the party.
"P.S. It's a beaut."

Both recess periods were taken up with arranging for the transfer of the dress to Henrietta. Vanessa wanted to walk out to Henrietta's house and deliver it at the door.

Henrietta didn't want that! She realized Tillie and Pa would have to know about the dress sometime. But not the dress *and* Vanessa at the same time. "It's too far," she objected.

"I don't mind," said Vanessa. "I walk a lot. Sometimes I walk just to be doing somethin'."

"I know what!" Henrietta thought of something. "When we come to town tomorrow afternoon, I'll walk over to your Aunt Belle's house and get it."

Vanessa looked scared. "Nobody'd be home. Aunt Belle'd be working. The house'd be locked."

"Nobody locks houses in Prairie Springs," said Henrietta, surprised. "Nobody takes things here."

But Vanessa just looked more scared than ever.

It was finally settled that Vanessa would meet Henrietta at Mrs. Swensen's when she delivered the eggs.

"But sometimes we don't get off on time," worried Henrietta.

"It don't matter. I'll wait."

"Don't wait in front of Mrs. Swensen's," said Henrietta. "She'll call out, 'What're you doing out there, little girl?' "

"I won't," promised Vanessa.

Saturday afternoon, when Henrietta turned onto Mrs. Swensen's street, she saw that Vanessa, true to her promise, was waiting at the end of the block, a good ways from Mrs. Swensen's.

Vanessa excitedly waved a large paper grocery bag in the air. Henrietta waved back. She had to keep waving because Vanessa kept waving.

But when Henrietta came out of Mrs. Swensen's house, Vanessa was up on the steps. "Here it is!" she cried and pulled a green dress out of the bag.

Henrietta glanced in alarm at Mrs. Swensen's windows. "Not here! Wait 'til we've turned the corner!"

Vanessa reluctantly shoved the dress back into the bag. "Just wait 'til you see it!"

A few steps before they reached the corner, the dress was out again. "Ain't it a beaut!" exclaimed Vanessa, holding it up for Henrietta to see.

But Henrietta wasn't looking. Her eyes were on Roland DeRuyter, who had just turned the corner and was coming toward them. She knew, of course, that his pa's house was in the next block. But she certainly hadn't expected to see *him* here. "Put it back," she hissed at Vanessa.

Vanessa disappointedly stuffed the dress back into the bag. "Don't you like it?"

"Yes, but I don't want *him* to see it," whispered Henrietta as Roland brushed past, his eyes unseeing.

"He's in our room, ain't he?" said Vanessa, looking back at Roland.

"He was sneering at us," said Henrietta with annoyance and pulled at Vanessa's hand to get her moving. It was beginning to seem that just let there be a bad time for Roland to appear—and there he was!

On the way back to Main Street, Vanessa kept peeking into the bag and smiling at the dress inside. "It's silk crepe," she said. "I'll bet you're the only girl at the party in silk crepe."

"I won't square dance lest I get it sweaty," said Henrietta.

"It's OK. You can dance," said Vanessa magnanimously.

"I won't drink punch lest I dribble on it."

"It's OK. You can drink punch."

Henrietta fell into silence. There was something she must say to Vanessa. But she didn't quite know how to say it. The car was in sight when she blurted out, "Don't tell nobody I'm wearing your dress!"

"I won't," said Vanessa agreeably.

That worry taken care of, Henrietta thought of something she hadn't thought to worry about before she got the dress. What would Pa say to her wearing a *borrowed* dress? She remembered that once the wheat had spoiled because the reaper broke and Pa wouldn't borrow one from a neighbor; he had tried to fix theirs, instead.

At the car, Vanessa didn't go away, as Henrietta wished she would. She just stood there smiling and smiling.

What would Aunt Tillie think of Vanessa? The reason safety pins were sticking out of Vanessa's dress was that all the buttons were missing.

"You don't need to wait," Henrietta said, and took the grocery bag from Vanessa's hand.

"I don't mind."

The reason Vanessa's dress was longer in the back than in the front, Henrietta noticed, was that the hem was out. "But you don't *need* to!"

Vanessa's smile grew very big. "Heck, I ain't got nothin' else to do."

Were Vanessa's lips really that red? Or had she got hold of her ma's lipstick? "I don't think you should be here when Pa and Aunt Tillie get back. I'm not supposed to be fooling around when we go to town," said Henrietta. She got in the car, closed the door, and busied herself with counting the egg money in the pail. When she looked up, Vanessa was far down the street, walking fast, her arms swinging furiously at her sides.

Now she's sore, thought Henrietta.

Suddenly Pa and Aunt Tillie were at the car.

"When you see the bargains I got, you'll see why it took me so long." Aunt Tillie was explaining to Pa as she climbed in with a big bundle in her arms.

Henrietta knew she must tell about the dress right away. The party started at seven-thirty—only two and a half hours away.

But she put it off until Pa got through town traffic. And out on the highway, Aunt Tillie kept pulling out bargains to show Pa, yelling to be heard above the rattling of the car.

It wasn't until the car slowed to make the turn into the driveway that Henrietta yelled—though a natural voice was what she wanted—"I'm invited to Eunice Anderson's party at the country club tonight at seven-thirty!"

There was a surprised silence up front.

Then Aunt Tillie said, "That dress you got on ain't clean enough for a party. I guess I got time to wash it out. I can iron it dry. But the purple'd be better. It looks more like a party dress."

"It looks like a woman's dress!" There she was yelling again. Henrietta dropped her voice. "I got a dress. Somebody who's not going is letting me wear hers."

"Clara?"

"Somebody else."

"Who?"

"A new girl. A town girl. Nobody you know." Henrietta took the dress out of the bag and passed it up to Aunt Tillie.

"Mercy!" exclaimed Aunt Tillie. "It's silk crepe! I can't wash it out if you get it dirty."

"I won't."

The car chugged to a stop. Pa got out and went straight to the barn instead of going inside first to change his shoes. Aunt Tillie and Henrietta sat looking at the dress.

"It's the latest style," said Aunt Tillie, holding it up so she could see on all sides. "I was in Butters' Dry Goods looking at patterns this afternoon, and they was showing leg-o' mutton sleeves and pleats in the back. And ain't them little rhinestone bows down the front pretty?"

Henrietta was awe-struck. She put out a

finger and touched the dress. The feel of the soft crinkle gave her goose bumps. She wished it wasn't green, though. Any color but green or purple.

"Mercy!" exclaimed Aunt Tillie. "Here we sit! And you due at that party. I better baste this hem up."

"You don't have to do nothin' to it!" Henrietta wanted the dress back. But Aunt Tillie had a tight hold on it.

"I'll bet my bottom dollar it's too long," said Aunt Tillie, grunting, as she struggled to get herself out of the car with her bundle in one hand and the dress in the other.

The dress was too long—way too long.

"Your friend must be a tall girl," mumbled Aunt Tillie, her mouth full of pins.

Henrietta, standing up on the stool so Aunt Tillie wouldn't have to bend, looked down and couldn't see anything of her legs but her ankles. It *couldn't* be Vanessa's dress! It had to be her ma's! At any moment—perhaps at this very moment—Vanessa's ma might look into the closet and say, "Where's my dancing dress?"

Henrietta wanted to tear the dress off and run. But she was stuck up on the stool.

"All done," said Aunt Tillie. Henrietta

hopped down from the stool. She pulled the dress over her head so fast Aunt Tillie shrieked, "You're gonna lose the pins!"

Aunt Tillie settled herself at the table, and Henrietta felt too unnerved to know what to do. She bet Vanessa didn't even have a party dress! She bet the whole time Vanessa was bluffing! She went around the kitchen in circles straightening rugs.

Pa came in from the barn with the milk and glanced with disappointment at the stove, which was filled with pans of water heating for Saturday night bath, and nothing else. "What's to eat?" he asked.

"I can't sew and cook both," muttered Aunt Tillie, biting off a thread.

"I'll cook supper," volunteered Henrietta, glad for something to do.

"There ain't time to cook," said Aunt Tillie. "But there's bread I baked this morning, and some of my strawberry jam, and fresh milk."

Aunt Tillie, still basting, shooed them away from the table. "I can't have eating near this silk crepe," she said.

So Pa and Henrietta drew their chairs up to the cupboard, pushed aside the milk crocks, and made room for their plates and cups. The lamp was at the opposite end of the room. Its light barely reached the cupboard. They ate in silence. Pa looked wrapped up in his thoughts—sad thoughts they seemed.

Henrietta made a little stab at cheerfulness. "The wind's stopped," she remarked. "Ain't that lucky? Now we won't get our hair mussed."

She got no answer and gave up, not being in an especially joyful mood herself. There was a scared little flutter somewhere in the vicinity of her heart that wouldn't go away.

"There now!" said Aunt Tillie, getting up from the table. "It's all done but for the pressing."

Henrietta jumped up and carried her plate to the sink.

"Let the dishes go," said Aunt Tillie. "You get the washtub ready for baths."

Henrietta was emptying a pan of boiling water into the tub when it occurred to her: It's an expensive dress. Vanessa's folks are poor. It must be Aunt Belle's dress. This was such a frightful possibility, Henrietta froze, bent over the tub.

Aunt Tillie looked up from the ironing board. "Somethin' wrong with the water in the tub?"

Henrietta straightened with a start. "Nothin'."

"You was staring at it like there was."

When the tub was filled, Aunt Tillie said to Henrietta, "You first. This is your night."

Henrietta had never sat in hot water before. Grownups went first. That's the way it was when Pa and Aunt Tillic were kids. So that's the way it was now. By her turn the water had cooled off. She'd no idea sitting in hot water felt so good.

Soaking in the hot water, Henrietta couldn't believe anything terrible was going to happen to her. Vanessa would never dare take Aunt Belle's dress. At worst, it was Vanessa's ma's. After Aunt Belle, Vanessa's ma didn't seem so fearsome.

And when Henrietta was all dressed, and Aunt Tillie said to Pa, "Don't she look nice?" and Pa answered, "Looks just like her ma." Henrietta felt a little rush of happiness and could hardly wait for the girls to see her in the dress.

CHAPTER 7

The car wouldn't start. Pa cranked and cranked. Aunt Tillie sat at the steering wheel working the choke and the spark and the gas lever and the ignition. She looked as if she had ten hands as they flew from one thing to the other. Henrietta, perched on the edge of the back seat, bit her finger nails in anxiety.

Suddenly her fright was back in full force. Vanessa *would* dare take Aunt Belle's dress! If Henrietta wouldn't be her friend unless Vanessa lent her a dress, Vanessa would dare anything, she was that desperate to keep a friend.

Henrietta wanted to cry out, "Don't start the car! I don't wantta go!" But after spending so much time fixing the dress, what would Aunt Tillie say to that?

The motor sputtered, hiccupped, and began to shake violently. Pa raced around to the driver's side and climbed in so fast Aunt Tillie barely had time to roll out of the way. Pa stepped on the gas pedal, and they were off!

No one talked. Pa's eyes were fixed on the road. So were Aunt Tillie's.

"Slow down," Aunt Tillie said. "There's a washboard spot up ahead."

Pa, who didn't like to be told how to drive, kept going at the same speed. When they hit the washboard spot, the heads up front jerked up and down, and Henrietta slid off the seat.

"You don't never listen to nobody!" Aunt Tillie scolded.

Thinking Aunt Tillie and Pa were about to quarrel over Pa's driving, Henrietta stayed down on the floor.

But there was only silence.

Henrietta picked herself up and got back on the seat, sitting with her head resting against the window. The jiggling of the pane was unsettling. But at the same time there was a familiarity about it, something that went back into her past, something that soothed. Nothing bad's gonna happen, she told herself, and believed it.

Off to the side she could see the lights of the town. On Saturday nights the stores stayed open until ten o'clock. And on Saturday nights the high school kids came to town. They went to the movies and to the dance hall. And here she was, going to a Saturday night party herself! It just went to show how close she was to being a high schooler.

Yet when the country club loomed into sight, Henrietta felt as if her stomach had dropped out of her.

"Now you notice everything so you can tell us all about it when you get home," said Aunt Tillie as the car slowed.

The car made a turn—stopped abruptly. The lights had picked up a sign at the entrance. "Members Only."

"You can get out here," said Pa.

Henrietta understood that Pa was offended by the "Members Only." She wished she'd thought to bring along the invitation. Maybe with it in her hand she wouldn't have this feeling of being where she wasn't supposed to be.

"Now you call us when you're ready to come home," said Aunt Tillie.

"Maybe I won't stay very long," said Henrietta, hopping down from the running board.

"You call us when you're ready!" shouted Aunt Tillie as the car pulled away.

No one was about. Not a soul in sight. She was late, of course. Still, she'd have thought there'd be somebody. She looked in panic after the departing car. It was picking up speed, the tail lights growing smaller and smaller in the darkness. Somewhat hesitantly, she began the walk up the gravel driveway. The crunch of her shoes in the loose pebbles was the only sound in the night.

There were nine steps going up to the veranda. She counted as she climbed. At the top she hesitated. Maybe she ought to sit awhile. Sort of catch her breath. But the weather-bleached chairs looked hard as bone in the moonlight. "Members Only," they seemed to be saying. She opened the door and stepped inside.

She found herself in a sitting room. No one was in it. Voices came from a door at the far side. The room wasn't as special a room as she'd expected. It looked the worse for wear. Once upon a time the red carpeting must have been very grand. But the tread of feet had made it dingy. There was a bare spot at the door.

The thing that caught Henrietta's fancy was a large mirror that hung over the fireplace. Stepping back all the way to the wall, she could see herself from head to foot.

She thought the dress beautiful. But her shoes were wrong. They looked shabby. She turned away from the mirror and went to the door from which the voices came. But when she reached it, she drew back. She'd gone as far as as she could go.

The door suddenly opened. Mr. Anderson breezed into the room. He picked up an ashtray, saw Henrietta, and said, "Aren't you coming in?"

"Ya," said Henrietta and followed him in.

She stepped into a large room nearly bare of furniture. The few chairs had been pushed against the wall, leaving the floor empty. In front of her was a long table around which her schoolmates stood bunched—a girl bunch and a boy bunch. Each bunch appeared unaware of the other bunch.

At the end of the table closest to Henrietta Mr. Anderson busily filled glasses from a punch bowl. At the other end were platters of cookies, over which Mrs. Anderson stood guard. She's counting how many you take, Henrietta suspected.

Henrietta was afraid of Mrs. Anderson, who

didn't like it if you came into her dress shop and just looked around and didn't buy anything. And once when Henrietta was standing on the sidewalk with her nose flattened against the pane, Mrs. Anderson came to the window and tapped on it, motioning for Henrietta to move on. I won't take but one cookie, decided Henrietta.

Henrietta's eyes fell on a chair partially hidden behind Mrs. Anderson. The chair was heaped with presents.

She forgot it was a *birthday* party! Henrietta didn't know what to do with her empty hands, which seemed, suddenly, the most obvious things in the room.

"Henrietta!" cried out a surprised voice. It was Clara, coming out of the girl bunch to meet Henrietta. Ruby was at her side.

"Where's your present?" asked Clara.

"I forgot."

"I don't see how you forgot *that!*"

Henrietta looked down in consternation, only to have her eyes fall on her shabby shoes. She right away moved into the middle of the girl bunch where they wouldn't be so noticeable. Suddenly she was face to face with Eunice.

"That one of the Johnson girls' dresses?" asked Eunice with a sour expression.

"Their things was all years old. This is the latest style. It's got leg o' mutton sleeves, and pleats in the back, and rhinestones down the front," said Henrietta. "And it's silk crepe," she added proudly.

Eunice wrinkled her nose in disdain. "It's a woman's dress. Girls don't wear silk crepe."

Henrietta at once felt utterly dreadful-looking.

And then Margy, Eunice's best friend, said, "That dress makes your eyes green."

And Beth said, "I love your eyes!"

And Amy added, "You got such long lashes."

Henrietta wasn't used to compliments. And from Eunice's group, too! She lowered her eyes in embarrassment. Then quickly raised them. It wouldn't do to look embarrassed. But then—just as she was beginning to feel pleased—Eunice, whose eyes had never left the dress, said, "I've seen that dress somewhere."

That alarmed Henrietta. She tried not to look alarmed.

"I bet it's not hers," said Margy.

"Maybe she rented it," suggested Amy.

"I know a place in Clara City that rents out wedding stuff," joined in Beth.

The switch from admiration to suspicion was so sudden it made Henrietta catch her breath. She gave her head a toss, it felt like a jerk, and said, "I wouldn't wear old rented stuff."

"Where did you get that dress!" came from somewhere behind Henrietta.

There was something menacing in the question—chilling. Henrietta was aware of eyes turning to see who'd said it. She kept her own eyes straight ahead.

A hand took hold of her shoulder and spun her around. She looked up into the outraged eyes of Mrs. Anderson.

"That dress was missing when I took inventory this evening!" Mrs. Anderson grimaced. "Now we know who took it, don't we?"

Mrs. Anderson didn't know. But Henrietta did! Not in her worst imaginings had she ventured on anything this terrible. She felt as if she'd been hit on the head with a hammer. She couldn't seem to think. Nor speak. Nor even move. She could only stand there and stare dumbly into Mrs. Anderson's accusing eyes.

"You took it, didn't you?"

The chatter about the table stopped.

"Answer me!"

But Henrietta couldn't.

"Harold," called Mrs. Anderson, letting go

of Henrietta to look for Mr. Anderson, who'd stayed with the punch.

Freed of Mrs. Anderson's eyes, Henrietta looked wildly about for help; though who could help her, she had no idea.

A circle of eyes stared back like fingers pointing at her. She dropped her eyes to the floor. A circle of shoes pointed at her.

Mr. Anderson's shoes joined Mrs. Anderson's satin pumps. Mr. Anderson was an important man. He was mayor of the town, and it was rumored he was running for state legislature. But his shoes were ordinary looking, a little rundown at the heel. Their ordinariness made them look friendlier than the other very new shoes surrounding her shabby pair. Henrietta fastened her eyes on them.

"Don't you know it's stealing to take a dress without paying for it?" said a man's voice, seeming to come from the shoes themselves.

Henrietta's eyes left the shoes and found a cookie that had been dropped. The thought popped into her head that if she could pick up the pieces without anybody noticing, she could eat them and it wouldn't count as her cookie. What an odd thing to be thinking at a time like this! But then something odd was happening to her head. The room, the people standing around her, all seemed not quite real. Not as unreal as a nightmare, more as if this couldn't be happening to *her*, and so must not be happening at all.

If you won't talk, there's nothing to do but call the sheriff," said Mrs. Anderson.

The sheriff! That jerked Henrietta back into reality. The sheriff took thieves to jail! Her eyes came up from the floor, looked in terror at Mrs. Anderson, saw no relenting there, turned in terror to Mr. Anderson.

Mr. Anderson placed a hand on Mrs. Anderson's arm. "Go slow, Gertrude," he said in a low voice. "The Hanson's are known as honest folk. Let's not start trouble."

"They're going to have to pay for the dress!" said Mrs. Anderson in outrage.

Pay for it! How could they do that when they had no money? Henrietta found her voice, a little of it, anyway. "You can have it back."

Mrs. Anderson drew herself up with indignation. "I don't sell second-hand things! It's your dress now. Your pa and your Aunt Tillie will have to make good on it."

There flashed before Henrietta the picture of Pa and Aunt Tillie sitting at home waiting for her call, waiting to hear "all about it." The picture was not bearable! It simply was not bearable!

All around her Henrietta could hear muttering. She heard, "Put on such airs, and all the time she stole it." And she heard, "Now I know where my new pencil disappeared to."

Henrietta's feet suddenly loosened themselves from the floor. She bolted through the crowd and out of the room, through the sitting room, down the steps of the veranda, out onto the highway.

A frightened glance over her shoulder revealed no one in pursuit. Still she ran. She ran past the town lights, out into the open country.

She ran until her gasping lungs would take in no more air. When she came to a stop beside a mailbox, she had to lean on it for support. Finally she could breathe more easily, and she straightened and stepped away.

The silk of her skirt clung to the wooden post. The dress was hateful to her! Nevertheless, it would have to pass inspection at home. She pulled it loose and tucked it in her bloomers for safe keeping.

The house belonging to the mailbox was dark, everybody in bed. How silent the countryside was on a windless night. But not a friendly silence. She felt a silence of condemnation.

They'd be sorry! When they found out it was Vanessa who took the dress, then they'd be sorry they shouted at her and stared at her and whispered about her!

But why hadn't she told it was Vanessa who took the dress? Henrietta shook her head over her folly. Now, even when they learned it wasn't she, they might go back to thinking it was. Like in school when you learned something wrong, and got corrected, and after a while got mixed up and went back to thinking the first thing was right.

Pa's good name! Such misery swept over Henrietta she wrapped her arms about her and rocked back and forth. She'd taken Pa's good name away! It was gone for good. From now on, people would hear the Hanson name, and they would say, "Wasn't there something about the Hansons? Something about a stolen dress?"

Yet how could she tell Mrs. Anderson out in front of everybody that Vanessa took the dress? Vanessa wouldn't have done it if it hadn't been for her. If only, only she hadn't told Vanessa she wouldn't be her friend unless she lent her the dress! In her anguish, Henrietta let out a little moan.

A rustling in the weeds in the deep ditch that ran alongside the highway sent her wheeling around. But it was dark down in the ditch, and the weeds were high.

And just then she saw car lights coming

down the highway, probably a farm family headed for home. They'd stop and want to know what she was doing out on the highway at night. She started walking up the driveway toward the house, as if she belonged there.

As soon as the car passed, she ran back to the highway. The gravel road was white in the moonlight. She could see almost as far down it as in daytime. There was nothing in sight. She headed for home, running at a trot that wouldn't wind her. She went from mailbox to mailbox. If she saw car lights, she turned up into the driveway and waited for the car to go by.

She was on the long stretch between the Johnsons' mailbox and her own when she heard a car coming up behind her. She skidded down into the ditch.

When her feet hit bottom, she instantly stopped dead still—just as she was, half crouching—her heavy breathing her only movement. Something was in the ditch with her! Something rustling the weeds! Abruptly the sound stopped. She strained to hear. But there was only the car as it slowly approached and then passed.

The car had scarcely gone by when Henrietta was clambering up the steep embankment. She stood on the highway for a moment listening. The air was so still and dry every sound reached her distinctly. But all that was there was the faint hum of the disappearing car. She heard *no* sound down in the ditch.

She began to think it was only a small animal she'd scared up.

She trotted on, alert for any sound outside of the steady clop, clop of her shoes on the gravel. Did she hear something? A sort of echo of her own steps? She stopped suddenly. From down in the ditch came the unmistakable sound of footsteps running through the weeds.

Henrietta fled in terror down the highway, running for her life. Still running at full speed, she turned into her driveway and was halfway up to the house before it dawned on her that no footsteps pounded after her. She nearly collapsed with relief. Her legs went rubbery, bending in strange directions. It was all she could do to steer them to the house.

At the door she slumped down on the step in a limp heap. The hammering of her heart in her heaving chest was painful.

As she sat there, the windmill began its gentle hum. The wind was picking up! The hostile silence of the night was broken. From the barn came the whinny of a horse. Immediately after it, a rooster crowed. Silly rooster! Mistaking moonlight for dawn.

Henrietta pressed her cheek against the cold, rough boards of the house. She was so very, very glad to be home. And it was the closest she could come to hugging her house.

No sound came from within. But the yellow light in the kitchen said very plainly, "We're up."

Henrietta crept to a window and peeped in. Aunt Tillie was fast asleep in the rocker, Pa on the floor. Now if she could just get in without waking them!

She took off her shoes. But the door was the problem. It squeaked. Opening it was like ringing an alarm. She inched it just enough ajar to squeeze through.

Pa gave an explosive snort, stopped snoring, and then, while Henrietta held her breath, got back into his rhythmic snoring.

Henrietta took off the dress and laid it across the table so Pa and Aunt Tillie would know she was home. Then she started up the stairs. They creaked. She took a step, listened, took a step, listened. It would be terrible to awaken them out of their sleep!

Groping in the darkness, she found her nightgown, slipped into it, crawled into bed, and turned her face to the wall.

She felt all at once that being accused of

stealing made her as bad as if she'd done it. How was she ever going to tell Pa and Aunt Tillie? She couldn't tell! But she'd *have* to tell! If she didn't, somebody else would. She wouldn't tell, though, until it got around it was Vanessa and not her. They wouldn't feel so bad then.

But with that thought, Vanessa was suddenly before her, smiling at everybody in sight. Vanessa would never get a friend now! And her pa would say, "Well, I tried staying put, and look what you did. The only thing to do is to keep moving."

And all because of her!

A tear rolled down Henrietta's cheek. She brushed it away. How silly to cry now when she didn't cry at all during the terrible part! But more tears came. She tried clenching her teeth and pinching her ears. Still the tears came. She got out of bed, went into Pa's little room, and knelt at the window. Below lay the moonlit barnyard.

"Junkyard!" Aunt Tillie called it.

But Henrietta didn't see junk. She saw fantastic shapes.

The broken wagon looked just like an enormous cow waiting at the granary door for a handout.

And the pump looked exactly like a boy;

Henrietta drew back with a start. The pump was a boy! Or rather, a boy stood hunched over the pump. He was looking up at the house.

The boy's face was in the shadow of his cap. Henrietta couldn't see it at all. Still, she thought she recognized Roland DeRuyter. The boy had Roland's height. And the way he stood hunched over the pump—as if he were leaning on cushions rather than hard iron—that was Roland's posture. Were those Roland's footsteps down in the ditch? But why?

Roland must have guessed the truth! He must have seen the dress come out of Vanessa's grocery bag. He must have heard their quarrel at the bus. But then, why did he let everybody think it was she? He must hate her, to just stand there and say nothing!

Looking at Roland slumped over the pump, Henrietta saw him in her mind slumping at his desk at the back of the room, the corners of his mouth pulled down in a sneer.

Her face grew warm with humiliation and indignation. Was Roland out there now watching the house with the same sneer, thinking the whole terrible fuss over the dress baby stuff?

She left the window and crawled back in bed. She was no sooner in, however, than she was out and back at the window. The pump was bare.

Had she imagined a boy at the pump? She hadn't imagined the footsteps in the ditch! She was sure of them! At least, she thought she was sure.

Doubting, Henrietta went back to bed. She fell into a fitful sleep. She heard steps on the stairs, but couldn't tell if they were going up or going down. She heard the lurch of Aunt Tillie's bed and thought Aunt Tillie must be getting into bed. But right away, or so it seemed, she heard pans rattling down in the kitchen. And it was morning.

Henrietta stayed in bed. The smells of breakfast came and went. Still she stayed in bed. She just laid there, scarcely moving.

It seemed hardly an hour had passed when she smelled dinner cooking. She smelled sausage and fried eggs and fried potatoes. The smell was irresistible. But she resisted it.

After dinner, the telephone began ringing. There were ten families on the party line. And Sunday afternoon was visiting time for farm families.

What if somebodys' telling about the stolen dress, and everybody's listening in? Henrietta thought.

Aunt Tillie wouldn't be listening. Aunt Tillie had her code of honor. She only listened late at night, after supper, anyway, and early morning. "Somebody might be needing help!" she explained.

Still, if a family received more than one call, Aunt Tillie might decide, "Maybe somethin's wrong!" and go for the receiver.

Henrietta stuffed her fingers in her ears.

Again it seemed as if no time at all had passed when Aunt Tillie was calling up, "Henrietta! It's two o'clock! You gonna sleep all day?"

"I'm awake."

"Whatcha doin' up there?"

"Resting."

"Come on down. I got your dinner kept warm on the stove."

Henrietta rested a little longer.

"It's three o'clock!" yelled Aunt Tillie from the foot of the stairs. "Come on down! It ain't good for you to lie in bed all day!"

Henrietta got up and made quite a bit of noise dressing so they'd know she was up and about. It was four o'clock when she got downstairs.

Pa and Aunt Tillie were seated at the table reading the *Weekly Prairie News*. Pa had one section, Aunt Tillie the other. They looked up expectantly at Henrietta. "Tell us all about it" was written all over their faces.

At the back of the stove Henrietta found a

plate heaped with sausage and fried eggs and fried potatoes. She sliced some bread and made a sandwich of the food, then ate standing beside the stove.

Aunt Tillie pointed to the chair next to her. "Sit down and tell us about the party."

"I can't eat and talk," said Henrietta, remaining at the stove.

"Did the DeRuyters bring you home? Old DeRuyter passed us on the way home, and I said to your pa, 'I best he's come from dropping off Roland.' We could of brung him if we'd of knowed. You must of gotten in late to of slept so long." Aunt Tillie looked questioningly at Henrietta.

Henrietta, her mouth full, said nothing.

"I set out that jar of my peach preserves to give to your friend's ma when I take the dress back next time your pa goes to town."

Some partly chewed bread and potato and sausage and egg sputtered across the room. "No! That'd embarrass her!"

"I don't see why. Seems like we oughta do somethin'."

"I gotta go feed the chickens," said Henrietta, stuffing what was left of the sandwich into her mouth.

"What'd they say about your dress?"

Henrietta pointed mutely at her bulging cheeks and went out the door.

The water tray was clogged with dirt. Henrietta had to clean it out before she could fill it. As she went about this chore, the chickens followed after her, getting in her way. She held out her hands to show them she had nothing. But they just gathered expectantly under her empty hands. Henrietta shooed them away in disgust. Aunt Tillie was right. Chickens didn't have the sense they were born with!

But later, after she'd fed them, as she stood among them using up time, Henrietta began to feel that chickens had a great deal of understanding. They scratched at the ground and cocked their heads at her and clucked as if to say, "See now, things can't be all that bad as long as there's still good things to be scratched up."

Henrietta felt somehow comforted.

CHAPTER 8

Henrietta woke in the morning feeling she'd swallowed something hard and cold. On the way to the bus stop she identified the feeling as fear of what the day held for her.

The bus was halfway to school before she remembered Roland at the pump. She turned and caught him looking—out of the window she sat beside, it might be supposed. For an instant their eyes met. Immediately they both looked away. But from that instantaneous encounter, Henrietta learned:

1. Roland knew it was Vanessa who had stolen the dress.
2. Roland followed her home.

3. Roland stood at the pump looking up at the house.

Just how one brief meeting of the eyes could tell her all this, Henrietta couldn't say. For a little while, she sat in a state of wonderment. Then a strange feeling came over her. All around her the bus was jumping with kids. Yet she had the feeling that she and Roland, just the two of them, each very aware of the other, sat alone in the bus. The feeling stayed with her the rest of the way to the schoolhouse.

Vanessa was in her seat. Henrietta looked as she came in the door. But Vanessa didn't see her. Vanessa's head was in a book. Several times during the morning, Henrietta looked back at Vanessa. But always Vanessa's head was in a book. The hard, cold lump inside Henrietta grew bigger.

At morning recess, Henrietta waited in the cloakroom for Vanessa. But Vanessa didn't see her waiting and whizzed by. When Henrietta got out of the cloakroom, Vanessa was up near the front of the line next to Clara and Ruby.

Out on the playground Vanessa was still with Clara and Ruby, who had her between them, as if to guard her. Henrietta didn't run after them. She stood up on the steps—in plain sight—where it would be easy for Vanessa to see her. But Vanessa didn't see her. Ruby and Clara sometimes glanced toward the steps. But not once did Vanessa look Henrietta's way.

And it struck Henrietta that she had no proof that it was Vanessa who took the dress.

And it struck Henrietta that it was too late now to tell on Vanessa. People would think she was trying to put the blame on Vanessa because she was a new girl.

Henrietta felt a squeezing inside her chest, making it hard to breathe. Vanessa was *not* going to tell!

The bell rang. Henrietta turned and faced the door. She heard a pounding of feet as the line formed behind her. The good thing about being first in line, she thought, is you can't see people looking at you.

And it struck Henrietta that this was the way it was going to be the rest of her life. In stores the clerks would stare and whisper, "We must keep an eye on that girl. She takes things." Life was done and over for her!

Henrietta didn't turn again in her seat to look at Vanessa. She kept her eyes to herself. Going down to the lunchroom, she looked at the floor. I'll sit by myself at the table, she determined. She had no problem. Nobody sat next to her.

When they went out for noon recess, Henrietta stood at the iron railing that separated the yard from the street. She was thinking: When Vanessa gets away from the school kids, she'll change her mind about not telling. Maybe if I run to meet her and get to her before Ruby and Clara . . .

Henrietta watched in vain. Vanessa did not return to school.

Back in her seat, Henrietta had a hard time with her schoolwork. Her mind didn't work right. There was a kind of fuzziness to it. She could pronounce the words in her books. But she could draw no meaning from them.

But on the bus, away from the schoolroom, nearing home, Henrietta's mind cleared. And it occurred to her that she did have proof! Roland knows it was Vanessa. He could tell everybody.

She looked back. As usual, Roland's eyes were out the window. His face wore a look of bored discontent. It didn't look like the face of somebody willing to go out of his way to help somebody else. The purple spot on his tan jacket seemed to grow bigger and brighter right before her eyes.

Henrietta turned front with a sinking heart. How did you ask somebody to help you when that person didn't like you?

Dread and worry were back in full force. Trudging up the driveway, she recalled Mrs. Anderson's words, "Your folks will have to pay for it!"

It was urgent that she tell Pa and Aunt Tillie about the dress right away, just as soon as she got in the house, before the Andersons got to them!

It was wash day. The clothes had been hung inside, out of the dusty wind. Clothes lines crisscrossed the kitchen.

Aunt Tillie stood bent over a washtub, her sleeves rolled up to her shoulders. The fat on her arms jiggled as she pumped her arms up and down. Her face was red. She looked cross.

From behind a sheet Henrietta heard the tinkle of shelled corn as it struck the tin pail. Pa was inside. But what was he doing hidden behind a sheet? Why wasn't he in his chair by the window? She lifted the sheet to get under it.

"Leave your pa alone," Aunt Tillie said to stop her. "He's had a bad day."

Was she too late? Had the Andersons got to them? Henrietta felt that her heart had quit beating.

Then Aunt Tillie explained, her voice rising with her anger. "Old DeRuyter had the gall to come over and say to your pa, 'I'm willing to give you thirty dollars an acre for that forty next to my fence.' Thirty dollars! That's robbery! Why, he was offering fifty dollars a few years back when times was better. He knows he's got us over a barrel, the old thief!"

"Ping, ping!" went the shelled corn behind the sheet, picking up speed.

Henrietta looked anxiously over at the sheet.

"Old thief, that's what he is!" Aunt Tillie kept on. "And Young DeRuyter—that elevator he's got a job with don't give no time at all to farmers who can't pay their storage. Them DeRuyters ain't nothin' but a pack of thieves!"

Henrietta wished Aunt Tillie would stop saying, "Thief." The word made her skin crawl. She suddenly wheeled and headed resolutely for the door.

"Where you going?"

"Just out."

"Don't go far. I'm gonna need you to help empty the tubs."

Across the barnyard Henrietta marched resolutely, across the wheat field, straight for the DeRuyter house. She'd bring no more trouble on Pa! It was her mess—and she'd get out of it herself!

But when she reached the DeRuyter cornfield, her steps grew less resolute. Once many years ago she had played in the DeRuyter cornfield. Old Mrs. DeRuyter, thinking a pig was in the corn, came running into the field, a broom raised above her head. Finding only a little girl, Mrs. DeRuyter had lowered the broom and said, "Vas you do hier, liddle mädchen?" Henrietta, scared out of her wits, had run for home. She hadn't come back since.

Today the corn was not so high. And she was taller. It did not block out the big white, square house with its many windows. Those windows, glistening in the late afternoon sun, seemed to be saying to her, "Vas you do hier, liddle mädchen?"

At the edge of the apple orchard, Henrietta's feet stopped altogether. She could go no farther. She could not go up to the door of that big white, square house and knock on it and ask for Roland.

A dog came running out of the open barn door, barking furiously. Henrietta turned and walked away. Pa had told her, "If a dog comes after you, don't run. Just walk slowly, like you wasn't scared. If you're scared, the dog can smell it."

But she *was* scared! And she was wondering if, in that case, it wouldn't be better to run, when somebody whistled to the dog and it stopped barking.

Henrietta kept walking, faster now that the

dog wasn't after her. But as she neared her house, it began to look as forbidding as the DeRuyters'.

What a bleak little house, with no trees around it at all. And how badly in need of paint! Whole strips along the front were gray where the paint had peeled off. And the boarded-up side had no paint at all. The house had a woebegone look about it, as if life had been hard and the future held nothing better.

Henrietta turned away from her house, turned toward the boulder at the edge of the cornfield. She headed for the boulder because she could think of nowhere else to go. But when she got there, it seemed that she had come with a purpose. Today she would climb to the top!

All her life she'd wanted to get to the top. Pa could do it. He just put his fingers in some grooves and hoisted himself up. But when Henrietta copied him, nothing happened.

"When you get big enough, then you can do it," Pa said.

Henrietta found the grooves and pushed and pulled and gave little hops. But she couldn't get to the top. She slumped to the ground. She was good for nothin'! She felt like crying, but was too worn out with failure for even that.

"Why do you want to climb it?"

Henrietta looked up in amazement. There

stood Roland DeRuyter. But a different Roland! The corners of his mouth weren't pulled down. They turned up in a sort of half smile. He didn't seem to want them to do that. He kept straightening them. But they would turn back up.

He's happy about something, realized Henrietta. She wondered if his grandpa had gotten him a pony. The first day of school Miss Hawes asked the class to write a theme on what they most wanted. Roland's was about a pony. It got tacked up on the bulletin board. Henrietta had read it while she was sharpening her pencil.

But this wouldn't do—sitting here staring as if she were afraid to turn her eyes lest he disappear! She got awkwardly to her feet. "So I can see things," she answered, and brushed the dirt off her dress.

"You can see farther from an upstairs window," said Roland, turning to the boulder, measuring it with his eye.

"It's not the same."

"I was in the barn, and I seen you in the orchard," he said, and shot her a questioning glance over his shoulder.

Ask him to tell about Vanessa! said a little voice inside Henrietta. Quick! Before he goes away!

But it wasn't as easy as the little voice seemed

to think. For one thing, Roland's attention was on the boulder. He was running his hands over it, feeling for the grooves.

And something else—Roland didn't look as if he'd come from barn chores. His blue shirt looked as if it had just been unwrapped from the store. And his very new-looking, very white sneakers had most certainly never been inside a barn. The string of one was tied in a knot, the other not tied at all.

It occurred to Henrietta that Roland would look the way he did if he'd run inside the house, changed his shirt and shoes, and then come running after her. This was such an interesting observation, it took all her attention.

Finding the grooves, Roland tried to hoist himself up, but only got far enough to see what was on top. He dropped to his feet and stood looking at Henrietta. He looked as if he wanted to say something to her.

Now! said the little voice.

Instead, Henrietta turned away from Roland—took several steps toward her house—realized that wasn't what she wanted to do—half stopped—but saw that Roland had fallen into step at her side—and so kept going.

It'll be easier to talk when we're doing something, she thought.

But walking, Roland appeared to have lost interest in talking. His toe picked up a hard lump of dirt, and his attention was on it. He kicked it along, kicking carefully so as not to shatter the dirt. The lump kept going sideways. And then Roland went after it, bringing it back with his toe.

Henrietta, watching the barn get closer and closer, was in despair. How could she possibly ask Roland to "tell," when he was darting all over the field?

All at once Roland dismissed the lump of dirt with a kick that sent it flying off in several pieces. He put his hands in his pockets, took them out to rub his ears, put them back in again. Then, out of the blue, he said, "You didn't tell."

Henrietta knew instantly what he meant. She stopped dead in her tracks and looked right at Roland. He stopped, too, and looked right at her.

If it flashed into Henrietta's mind that now was the time to ask Roland to "tell," the thought was put to rest by the look in Roland's eyes. His black eyes glowed with pride and pleasure.

"I bet there ain't one in ten thousand that wouldn't have told," he said, looking at her as if—impossible as such a thing must be—as if it were she, Henrietta herself, and not a pony or anything like that, who was making him happy.

Henrietta had seen that look before in Pa's eyes, when she remembered all her lines in the Armistice Day program, though she had the longest part and some with shorter parts forgot theirs. But she'd never seen such a look in the eyes of someone her own age. And Roland DeRuyter, of all people! It filled her with a pleasant excitement.

But then it seemed to her that Roland was looking at her as if he expected her to say something in response to what he'd said. And there wasn't, exactly, anything she could say. She started walking for home, rather fast.

Roland, hands jammed in his pockets, kept pace at her side.

Flustered, Henrietta stumbled over a furrow, caught herself.

A hand shot out, found itself unneeded, hastily returned to its pocket.

I'm being walked home, it occurred to Henrietta. Sometimes boys walked home with Eunice. But she hadn't supposed a boy would walk her home. And Roland DeRuyter, of all people! It was flattering. Yet what she most wanted—more than anything in the world, she suddenly felt—was to be able to run off from him.

When they reached the fence, Henrietta climbed right over it. She wasn't sure what you said to a boy who walked you home. Just, "so long." Or did you have to say something else? Whatever it was, it seemed easier to say it with a fence between them.

To her dismay, as her feet hit the ground, so did Roland's, right next to hers, on her side of the fence. He looked as if he meant to go all the way up to the house, to go inside, even.

"Goodby!" Henrietta blurted out. "I gotta go now!"

For a second—though it seemed much longer—Roland just stood there, no smile on his lips now, and looked into her panicky eyes. Then without a word he turned, sprang over the fence, and walked away, taking quick, hard strides.

Henrietta hung onto the fence, looking after him woefully. She'd said a dumb thing again. She'd hurt his feelings. And she hadn't wanted to. He wouldn't have anything more to do with her now. That's what his look said. It said, "OK. If that's the way you're going to be, I'm through with you."

Suddenly, unexpectedly, Roland looked back. He caught Henrietta looking after him, caught her looking utterly woebegone. It made him smile. Not a half smile. A whole smile, his black eyes sparkling with it. "Be seeing you," he said. And was off again, walking with a springy step, as if he'd like to leap up and touch the sky, and might have if he hadn't felt watched.

Henrietta stayed at the fence. The happiness she'd felt at Roland's smile disappeared as he disappeared. She was letting him get away without asking him to tell on Vanessa! Yet how could she ask him? But what was she to do now? Then darkness closed in, and she couldn't see him at all.

Darkness! The chickens hadn't been fed! She ran at once to the granary and dipped a pan into the oat bin. Then she ran to the chicken house, the wind blowing the oats up into her face.

The chickens had already gone to roost. She pushed them off the poles, chased them out of the house, and stood before the door, not letting them back in. "You can't come in 'til you've eaten!" she yelled at them.

But—stupid things!—they stayed in front of the door and tried to duck between her legs. In the end she had to let them go to bed hungry.

She trudged slowly up to the house, her feet dragging as if they carried balls and chains. It was all very well for Roland to think she was some kind of heroine. It didn't cost *him* anything. She didn't want to be a heroine! It was more fun to read about heroines than to be one. And yet she didn't want Roland to stop thinking she was one, either.

The tubs had been emptied and rolled against the wall. Aunt Tillie stood at the stove cooking supper. She looked up crossly. "Where you been?"

"Feeding the chickens."

"It don't take that long to feed chickens."

"What do you want me to do?"

"I want you to sit down at that table and do your homework! First thing you know, it'll be bedtime and you still at lessons."

Henrietta spread her school things out on the table. She opened her arithmetic book to the right page. But that done, she dropped her head into her hands. Her head felt too full of *real* problems to take on made-up problems. There was no way out! Tonight she *had* to tell Pa and Aunt Tillie about the dress.

The door opened, and Pa came in with the milk pails, bringing the smell of the barn with him. Aunt Tillie at once began setting the table. "Supper's ready," she announced.

Full of dread, Henrietta took her place. Eating put Pa and Aunt Tillie in their best mood. Now was the time to tell them. But how satisfied with life they looked as they filled their mouths! Let them enjoy their supper, she decided.

Supper over, Henrietta stacked the dishes in the dishpan. She took a kettle from the stove and poured hot water into the pan. Then she rubbed the bar of soap between her hands to make suds.

Aunt Tillie sat with her swollen feet in a pan of cold water. Her head began to nod.

Pa picked up a harness from the corner by the door and brought it over to the table to mend it under the lamplight. But pretty soon the harness dropped unattended to his lap. He sat staring sadly out into the night.

A dreary stillness settled over the kitchen, the only sounds the swish of dishwater and clink of a dish. Then came Aunt Tillie's little whistle. Henrietta glanced over her shoulder. Aunt Tillie was fast asleep.

Good. It would be better to tell only Pa. Then when she was in school tomorrow, Pa could tell Aunt Tillie.

Henrietta dried her hands and went over to Pa. She put one hand on his shoulder, and with the other gently rubbed at his furrowed brow, though she knew from having tried it before that rubbing did no good.

She looked about for something cheerful to use as a starter. She saw only wet clothes within and black night without.

"You wouldn't guess it's bright outdoors, with moon and stars," she chirped. "With the lamp lit, it just looks black out there, don't it?"

Pa patted the hand that lay on his shoulder, in that way letting her know he heard her, but wished to be left alone just now.

Henrietta went back to the dishes. The dishrag dragged slowly back and forth. She was thinking that she couldn't tell Pa about the dress. She just couldn't. Anything would be better than telling Pa. Even asking Roland to tell on Vanessa would be better.

She'd do it tomorrow! She'd come right out and say to Roland, "The reason I was in your orchard was because I wanted to ask you to tell everybody it was Vanessa who took the dress and not me."

Roland would despise her! He would ask with a sneer, "Why me?"

She would answer, "Because you're the one who heard me tell Vanessa at the bus I wouldn't be her friend unless she lent me her dress."

No, she'd better not say that.

She would say, "Because I'm afraid nobody will believe me if I tell."

What a coward, Roland would think. He would turn without a word and stride away.

She couldn't ask Roland to tell. She just couldn't!

Whatever was she to do?

CHAPTER 9

It seemed to Henrietta that she woke up feeling angry. Though perhaps it was while she was dressing that the anger welled up. She wasn't going to let Vanessa get away with this! She would confront her! Shame her! Make her tell! By the time Henrietta went downstairs, her anger was so great she choked on breakfast.

When she got on the bus, Henrietta raised her eyes just enough to see that Roland was on it. Then she ignored him. She wished—at least, at this moment she wished it—that they hadn't kept bumping into each other the way they had. Somehow, though she didn't know exactly how, a sort of bond seemed to have established itself between them. And she wanted to cut herself loose.

Clara and Ruby stood waiting where the buses pulled up in front of the schoolhouse. Henrietta was afraid they had something mean to say to her. She rushed past them.

"Wait! We got something to tell you!" Ruby called after her.

Henrietta paid no attention.

"Vanessa's run away!"

Henrietta stopped running and walked slowly so the two girls could catch up. She was shocked. How could she make Vanessa tell if Vanessa was gone?

Clara came panting up first. "Half the town's been out all night looking for her!"

"They think maybe she's hopped a freight!" added Ruby, catching up.

"That's a good way to see the country cheap," said Henrietta, her heart hard.

When she entered the room, Henrietta was too upset over losing Vanessa to notice that Miss Hawes was acting strangely. But in her seat, Henrietta observed that Miss Hawes wasn't at her usual place at the board putting up work. Miss Hawes sat stiffly at her desk watching her pupils come into the room. She didn't look as if she liked them very much.

*

Rollcall over, Miss Hawes looked grimly at her class and said, "I'm happy to report that Vanessa was found this morning in a haystack. She is unhurt."

There was a sort of gasp, like forty-two breaths being taken in at once.

Miss Hawes stood up. "Vanessa's father came to see me this morning. He gave me a note Vanessa wrote. With his permission, I'm going to read it to you."

Miss Hawes picked up a scrap torn from a paper grocery bag and read:

> *"Dear Ma and Pa,*
>
> *I done something bad. I took a dress out of a store to give to Henrietta, who is my very best second-best friend I ever had. She don't know nothing about it. I'm sorry I caused so much trouble so I'm running away.*
>
> *Vanessa*
>
> *P.S. Don't look for me."*

The room was so still it was as if even breathing had been suspended.

Miss Hawes just stood there frowning at her class. Her class began to stir uneasily.

"I'm going to tell you a story," said Miss Hawes at last, "about myself when I was a girl."

Her class relaxed. There was even a little ripple of excitement. Miss Hawes didn't tell stories. And now a story about herself!

"My mother didn't believe in spending money on clothes," began Miss Hawes in her teaching voice, sounding more as if she were giving out an assignment than telling a story. "My clothes were very plain. I envied those whose clothes were nicer than mine and looked down on those whose clothes were worse."

Miss Hawes paused to see the effect of this on her class. Again her class stirred uneasily. It was clear that this story was not "for fun."

"There was a girl on my block whose dresses were always torn and dirty," continued Miss Hawes. "One day I heard a furious barking in my back yard. I ran out and saw that two dogs had cornered my cat. I stood there, screaming with horror. Suddenly the girl in the torn dress ran right into the midst of the snapping, snarling dogs, picked up my cat, and brought her to me."

Again Miss Hawes paused to look at her class. Then she went on, speaking more slowly, picking her words carefully, as if to make sure every word was understood. "From then on I saw the ragged girl with different eyes. I saw her courage. It made me wonder if I could see other people with different eyes. Sometimes I could. Sometimes what I saw was sad. But once having seen with different eyes, I wanted to see that way always."

Miss Hawes stopped. Her eyes roamed the room, seemingly searching for something. Apparently she didn't find it. A shade of disappointment passed over her face, and something sorrowful, too. She sat down at her desk, and just sat there. Then she gave her head a little shake as if trying to figure out how to get something across. She gave up.

"Open your geography books to page thirty-two," she said, going back to the one thing she knew exactly how to do: teach the lessons that came out of books. And school began.

Henrietta sat with her head lowered in shame. She thought she understood what Miss Hawes meant. Miss Hawes didn't want you to care about dresses. She wanted you to care about things like courage. Henrietta was afraid Miss Hawes meant the story especially for her. Though once when Miss Hawes's severe eyes were roaming the room, they had paused for an instant on her and, for that instant, had softened.

Henrietta wiggled uncomfortably. If Miss Hawes knew *all,* Miss Hawes wouldn't look at her so benevolently. There was a missing part in Vanessa's note. The part about how Henrietta had said she wouldn't be Vanessa's friend unless she lent her the dress. Henrietta felt a great need to fill in the missing part for Miss Hawes.

As Henrietta put her books away for morning recess, she knew what she must do. She must stay in the cloakroom until the room was empty. Then she must come out and confess to Miss Hawes.

But the last steps had scarcely shuffled out of the room when suddenly Miss Hawes was looking in at her. It was a punishable breach of rules to hide in the cloakroom. Henrietta hadn't expected to be caught *in* the cloakroom. She'd expected to come out and announce herself. Caught, she felt as guilty as if hiding had been her intent.

"Henrietta! What are you doing in here?" said Miss Hawes, frowning.

Henrietta was too scared to answer.

Miss Hawes came in, took Henrietta's hand, and led her out of the cloakroom to her desk. Then she sat down, and taking both of Henrietta's hands in her own, said, "Do you want to tell me what's the matter?"

This was so kind, so understanding, that Henrietta burst into tears. Miss Hawes rummaged in a drawer and came up with a handkerchief.

Henrietta dried her eyes with it. But when

she tried to tell about the missing part, she burst into tears again.

Miss Hawes put her arm about Henrietta and said, "There, there."

That opened the floodgates.

Looking at wit's end, Miss Hawes said, "Why don't you go outside with the rest of the class? I think you'll find they think better of you than you suppose."

Henrietta went gratefully sobbing out of the room. She stopped at the girls' room and splashed cold water on her face. She hadn't gotten out the missing part. But then, Miss Hawes seemed to understand a lot of things without being told.

The crying under control, except for a left-over tear or two, Henrietta went outdoors and sat on the steps, watching the kids milling about the playground. She felt like a stranger. Well, not exactly a stranger. More as if she'd been away a long time, many months, and had just come back.

Ruby and Clara spotted her. They came running up, each taking one of Henrietta's hands, and paraded her out into the yard.

"You should of told us it was Vanessa," complained Ruby. "After all, what are friends for?"

Clara widened her eyes at Ruby. "Henrietta don't snitch on other kids!"

"I wonder if Vanessa will be let back in school," speculated Ruby. "Maybe they'll send her to reform school."

Just then somebody tapped Henrietta from behind. It was Eunice. "Come with me, Henrietta," she said. "Our group wants to talk to you."

Full of dread, Henrietta went along with Eunice. She didn't feel up to contending with Eunice's group. You needed your wits about you for that. And she felt too distracted to use her head just now.

The group was waiting. They closed in on Henrietta.

"You could have told me you didn't steal the dress," reproached Eunice. "We were best friends once back in third grade, you know."

"Vanessa only took it because I said I wouldn't be her friend if she didn't lend me her dress," said Henrietta. She was surprised at how easily it came out.

Eunice looked hard into Henrietta's eyes, as if trying her best not to see the cast-off dress and the scruffy shoes. "We took a vote," she said. "We want you in our group."

The impenetrable wall that enclosed the popular had opened. Henrietta was allowed to step inside. But it seemed to her that somehow she wasn't enjoying the privilege the way she should. A terrible suspicion that the only reason Eunice's group wanted her was because Miss Hawes's story made it the fashionable thing to do began to take root. If that's all it was, it wouldn't last long. Henrietta saw, stretching before her day after day, the worry: Will they tire of being "nice" to me today?

Before Henrietta could say anything, suddenly all eyes were turning away. Henrietta followed their gaze and saw Vanessa and her pa coming down the sidewalk toward the schoolhouse. Vanessa's pa held her hand tucked inside his own.

He took her a little way into the schoolyard and then turned and walked away. Henrietta watched his retreating figure for a moment. He walked with head bent, eyes on the ground.

Then Henrietta looked at Vanessa. Vanessa stood where her pa had left her, the toe of one shoe digging into the sandy ground. Her thin shoulders were hunched together, as if trying to hide the rest of her.

"The nerve of her coming back here," said Eunice.

"I'm not going to leave anything valuable in my coat pockets in the cloakroom anymore," said Margy.

"I got to go talk to Vanessa." Henrietta spoke up and stepped out of the circle.

The girls exchanged scandalized looks.

"Our group's not going to have anything to do with Vanessa," warned Eunice.

But Henrietta was on her way.

"You talk to Vanessa, you can't be in our group," Eunice shouted after her.

Henrietta scarcely heard. Her mind was busy as she walked across the school grounds. She was thinking that somewhere in the school yard, Roland DeRuyter was probably watching. And she was thinking that Miss Hawes might be looking out the window. Miss Hawes often took a look when the class was outdoors.

Vanessa, busily digging with her toe, didn't raise her head. She watched Henrietta's approach guardedly through her eyelashes. When Henrietta stopped in front of her, Vanessa looked up and smiled. But the only thing Henrietta could see was the fear in Vanessa's eyes.

"Want a second-best friend?" said Henrietta as she took Vanessa's hand.